She stretched her arms
toward the threatening sky,

Shifting her ribs experimentally around the soreness remaining from the long ride east. She had left Battlefox Demesne last year, had spent the intervening seasons in Schlaizy Noithn —trying, without success, to remedy an unpleasantness in that tricksy land—and had come out not long ago to Shift into her own shape and equip herself for the journey. So, horse legs instead of her own legs; real clothing instead of mere Shifting; her own face instead of the grotesqueries she had used lately. There was nothing Shifty about her now, nothing to betray her except the quivering Shifter organ deep within her which would announce the presence of another of her kind.

As it did now.

She crouched, ready to assume fangs and claws. There was no one on the road in either direction. She searched the dark forest from which a questioning howl rose, abruptly broken off. Her teeth lengthened slightly and her feet dug into the soil. . . .

Ace Fantasy Books by Sheri S. Tepper

THE REVENANTS

The Books of the True Game
KING'S BLOOD FOUR
NECROMANCER NINE
WIZARD'S ELEVEN
THE SONG OF MAVIN MANYSHAPED
THE FLIGHT OF MAVIN MANYSHAPED
THE SEARCH OF MAVIN MANYSHAPED

THE SEARCH OF MAVIN MANYSHAPED

SHERI S. TEPPER

ACE FANTASY BOOKS
NEW YORK

THE SEARCH OF MAVIN MANYSHAPED

An Ace Fantasy Book / published by arrangement with
the author

PRINTING HISTORY
Ace edition / September 1985

ISBN: 0-441-75712-X

Ace Fantasy Books are published by The Berkley Publishing Group,
200 Madison Avenue, New York, New York 10016.
PRINTED IN THE UNITED STATES OF AMERICA

Chapter 1

The season of storms had begun in earnest when Mavin Manyshaped rode down the Ancient Road, beneath the strange arches, toward the city of Pfarb Durim. It was almost twenty years since she had been there last; twenty years since she had promised to come there again. "The Blue Star hangs upon the horns of Zanbee," she sang to herself, not sure she was remembering it correctly. It was something Himaggery had said, was it? Something Wizardly, a specific time which had to do with the season and the arches? The tall horse she rode tiptoed into the shadow of each arch with shivering skin, dancing as he came out again, and she adjusted to this fidgety movement with calm distraction. Twenty years ago they had promised to meet upon the terrace of the hotel Mudgery Mont in the city. Looking down from this height upon the labyrinth of walls and roofs, she was not sure she could find her way to the hotel. Ah. Yes, there it was. Upon the highest part of the city, almost overlooking the cliff wall. She chirruped to the horse, urging him to stop fidgeting and move along.

Just beyond the last of the Monuments was a small inn, a dozen empty wagons scattered around it, as though parked there until the weather cleared, and a fork in the road with one branch leading down to the town. A distant rumble of thunder drew her attention to the clouds, boiling up into mountainous ramparts over the city, black as obsidian, lit from within by a rage of lightning and from the east by the morning sun. This was the weather during which the Monuments were said to dance. While it was never alleged that they had any malevolent intent, it was true that certain travelers caught on the Ancient Road during storms arrived at Pfarb Durim in no condition to pursue their business. If they had the voice for it, and unfortunately sometimes when they did not, they tended to lie about with unfocused eyes singing long, linear melodies which expressed a voice of disturbing wind. Mavin shivered as the horse had done, encouraging him to make better speed toward the distant gates.

A few she knew of had actually seen the Monuments dance. Blourbast the Ghoul had seen, only to die moments later with Huld's dagger in his throat. Huld the Demon and Huldra, his sister-wife had seen, as had their mother, Pantiquod the Harpy. Mavin spat to get the memory of them out of her mouth. She had heard they had gone away from Hell's Maw, left that warren beneath the walls of Pfarb Durim to inhabit another demesne: Bannerwell, beside the flowing river. It was, so her informant had said, a cleaner and more acceptable site for a Gamesman of power. Kings and Sorcerers who could not be enticed to Hell's Maw for any consideration would plot freely with Huld in Bannerwell. She spat again. The memory of him fouled her mind.

Two others had seen the Monuments dance, of course; Mavin, herself, and the Wizard Himaggery. They, too, had gone away separately after promising to meet again when twenty years had passed. Now Mavin Manyshaped rode her tall horse along that Ancient Road, so lost in memory of that other time she paid little attention to the clouds towering over the city. Two decades ago there had been wild drumming in the hills, a fury of firelight, and a flood of green luminescence from the dancing arches. The murmur of present thunder and the threatening spasms of lightning merely rounded out the memory.

A challenging shout brought her to herself. A gate guard, no less fat and lazy than those who had been here long ago. "Well, woman? I asked, were you bound into Pfarb Durim or content to sleep on your horse?"

"Bound in, guardsman. To Mudgery Mont."

He gave her a curious glance, saying without saying that he thought her a strange guest for the Mont. Most of those who stayed there came with retinues of servants or with considerable panoply. She gave him a quirky smile to let him know she read his thought, and he flushed slightly as he turned away. "Go then. The gates are open to all who have business within."

As indeed they always were, she reflected. There was no city in all the lands of the True Game so open, not even Betand, which was a crossroad itself. And, as in other of the commercial cities of the land, there was little large scale Game—though much small scale stuff, Games of two, family duels and the like—and a minimum of Game dress. Helmed Tragamors could be seen around the inns and hotels. Even here guards were often needed. A gaudy band of Afrits entered the square as she crossed it, bound away south, no doubt, to the Great Game lately called in the valley land beside Lake Yost, in the midland. Everyone had heard of that; the first Great Game in a decade and half. The Gamesmen in the land headed to it or from it, as their own needs struck them.

The streets were shrill with hawkers, bright with banners, alive with a smell she remembered, rich and complex, made of fruit both rotted and fresh, smoked meats, hides, the stink of the great cressets upon the wall full of grease-soaked wood. The pawnish people of Pfarb Durim had a distinctive dress; full black trousers thrust down into openwork boots (which let the dust and grit of the road sift in and out while somewhat hiding the dirty feet which resulted) and brilliantly colored full shirts with great billowy sleeves. The women belted these garments with an assortment of sashes and chains, topping all off with an intricately folded headdress; the men used simple leather belts and tall leather hats. Both sexes fluttered like lines full of bright laundry or a whole festival of pennants, and were shrill as birds with their cries and arguments. The tall horse picked his way through this riot fastidiously, ears forward, seeming interested in all that went on around him.

As she came farther into the city, the noise quieted, the smell dwindled, until, between the rumbles of thunder, she could hear the wind chimes and smell the flowers in the Mont gardens. The courtyard wall was surmounted with huge stone urns spilling blossoms down the inner wall where a dozen boys plied wet brooms to settle the dust, though by the look of the sky this task would soon prove redundant. The Heralds at the entry looked up incuriously, and then returned to their game of dice, dismissing her in that one weighing glance. "Of no importance," their eyes said. Mavin agreed with their assessment, content to have it so.

A liveried stableman came to take the horse, and she let him go thankfully. It was no easy matter to ride upon another's four legs where she could go easier upon her own. But Shifters were not always welcome guests, not even among Gamesmen notable in treachery and double dealing, so she came discreetly to the Mont, clad in softly anonymous clothing of sufficient quality to guarantee respect without stirring avarice or curiosity.

Now, she thought, I will meet him as I promised, and we will see. What it was she would see she had not identified. What it was she would feel, she had carefully avoided thinking of. Each time her mind had approached the thought it had turned aside, and she had let it turn, riding it as she might a wilful steed, letting it have its own way for a time, until it grew accustomed to her—or she to it. She went into the place, shaking her head at the man who would have taken her cloak, wandering through the rich reception halls toward the terrace she remembered. It lay at the back, over the gardens which stretched down to the cliff edge and the protecting wall, bright under their massed trees, their ornamental lanterns. The door was as she remembered it, opened before her by a bowing flunkey—

And she stood upon the terrace, shaken like a young tree in a great storm.

"Gameswoman?" She didn't hear him. "Gameswoman. Are you well? A chair, Madam? May I bring you something to drink?"

Evidently she had nodded, for he raced away, stopping to say something to some senior servant at the doorway, for that one turned to look at her curiously. She took a deep breath, grasped at her reason with her whole mind.

"Come now, Mavin," she said to herself in a stern, internal voice seldom used, always heeded. "This is senseless, dangerous, unlike you. Sit down. Take a deep breath. Look about you, slowly, calmly. Think what you will say when he returns, how you will set his curiosity aside. Now. He is coming. Careful, quiet."

He set the glass of wineghost before her and she took it into her hand, smiling her thanks. "I was here last many years ago at the time of the great plague," she said in a voice of calm remembrance. "It was a tragic time. We lost many dear to us. The memory caught me suddenly and by surprise. You are too young to remember." She smiled again, paid him generously, and waved him away.

At the door he spoke once more to the other man, shaking his head. The other man nodded, said something with a serious face, but did not look in her direction. So. All was explained. All was calm. She sipped at the wineghost, staying alert. No one was interested in her. The few on the terrace were talking with one another or admiring the gardens or simply sitting, looking at nothing as they soaked the last of the morning sun slanting below the gathering clouds. Was Himaggery among them? Had he seen her come out without knowing her?

She examined the others carefully, one by one, discarding each as a possibility. She knew what he would look like, had visualized him many times. And yet—could it be that plump-ish fellow by the wall? Perhaps it was. Her stomach knotted. Surely not. Not. No. He had turned toward her with his pursey mouth and heavy-lidded eyes. Not Himaggery.

One of the men by the stairs, perhaps? The tall, martial-looking man? "Silly," she said to herself. "He has a Sorcerer's crown. Himaggery, if he wore Gamesman's garb at all, would wear Wizard's robes." She finished the wineghost, stood up abruptly and left the terrace. She had been so sure that he would be here when she arrived, so sure. So certain.

Inside she dithered for a moment. She could wander about the place, spend half a day doing it, without knowing whether he was here or not. There was a simpler way.

"Your title?" demanded the porter, officiously blocking the door of his cubby. "Your title?"

"If there is a message for me," she said, "it will be addressed simply to Mavin. I am Mavin, and my title is my own business."

He became immediately obsequious, turning to burrow in the untidy closet among papers and packages, some of them covered with the dust of years. It was obvious that nothing was ever thrown away on the Mont. She was ready with significant coin when he emerged, the sealed missive in his hand. "Who brought it?" she asked.

His eyes were on the coin as he furrowed his face, trying to remember. "A pawn, Gameswoman. A lean, long man in a decent suit of dark clothes. Many lines in his face. A very sad face, he had. The air of a personal servant about him. He did not stay at the Mont, you understand. He just left the message with me, along with the payment for its safe keeping and delivery." He looked at the coin once more, his expression saying that the previous payment could not have been considered sufficient by any reasonable person. She flipped it to him, left him groveling for it in the dusty closet as she turned the packet in her hands. So. Not Himaggery. A message delivered by a man who could only be Johnathon Went, old Windlow's man. Windlow. Himaggery's teacher. Himaggery's friend.

The last of the morning light had gone and rain was falling outside. She found a quiet corner in one of the reception rooms, behind a heavy drapery which held away the cold. The note in the tough parchment envelope was not long.

"Mavin, my dear," it said. "I have no doubt you will be in Pfarb Durim, faithful to your promise. Himaggery will be there, too, if he can. If he is not, it is because he cannot, in which case you are to have the message enclosed. Over the years, each time he has left me to go on one of his expeditions he has left a letter with me for you. This one was left eight years ago. I am sending someone with further information. Please await my messenger upon the Ancient Road—where the Monuments danced. . . .

"I think of you often and kindly. My affectionate regard. Windlow."

It was sealed with Windlow's seal. Another letter lay within. She stuffed them both into the pocket of her cloak, rose abruptly and went out into the courtyard, shouting for her horse, though the threatened rain had begun. When he was brought to her, she mounted without word and clattered through the city, almost riding through the guards at the gate. The rain had become a downpour and the roadway ran with water, but she urged the horse into a splashing canter up the hill toward the crossroad. She would not, could not have stayed in Pfarb Durim another moment. The city seemed to swallow her. She needed a smaller scope, with trustworthy walls around her.

The tiny inn ghosted into existence through the slanting knives of rain. She shouted to bring a stable boy out of the barn; his mouth was half full of his lunch. Inside the inn she found a room, acceptably clean though sparsely furnished, with a fire ready laid upon the hearth. Food was brought, and beer, and then the kitchen girl was gone, the door shut behind her, and Mavin sat beside the fire with the unopened letter in her hand.

"Well," she said. "Well and well. So all this hurry was for nothing, Himaggery. All this long ride from Schlaizy Noithn, this Shifting into acceptable form with an acceptable face and acceptable clothing. All for nothing. Nothing." Her thumb nail moved beneath the seal. It broke from the paper with a brittle snap, flying into the fire to sizzle upon the wood, hissing like a snake. "For nothing?" she said again, opening the page.

Mavin, my love:

Though I have called you my love often in these past seasons, you have never heard me. If you read this, the chance is great that this is the only time you will ever hear me.

I am going into the Northlands tomorrow, first to see the High Wizard Chamferton—who, I am told, knows much of the true origins and beginnings of things which have always intrigued me—and then farther north into places which are rumored often but seldom charted. There is a legend—well, you probably are not much interested in such things. If you were here now, Mavin, I would not be interested in them either.*

Since it is not likely you will read this—I have been, after all, fairly successful at looking after myself for some dozen years—I will allow me to say the things I could not say to you if you were here for fear of frightening you, sending you off in one shape or another, fleeing from me as you fled from Pfarb Durim so long ago. I will say that you have been with me each morning and each night of the time between, in every branch which has broken the sky to let sunlight through, in every deep-eyed animal I have caught peering at me in the forests, in each bird cry, each tumult of thunder. I will say that the thought of you has held me safe in times of danger, held me soft in times of hardship, held me gently when I would have been more brutal than was wise or fair.

Mavin, if I am gone, treasure how deeply I loved you, how faithfully, how joyously. Live well.

Yours as long as I lived,
Himaggery.

She sat as one frozen into stone, eyes fixed on nothing, the room invisible around her. So she sat while the food chilled and the fire died; so she sat until the room grew cold. "Ah, Himaggery," she said at last. "Why have you laid this on me, and you not here."

She rode out at dawn, spending the day upon the Ancient Road, waiting for Windlow's messenger. That day she did not eat, nor that night. The next day she ate something, though without appetite, and stayed again upon the road. The third day she told herself would be the last. If Windlow's messenger did not come, then no messenger would come, and she would ride south to Tarnoch to talk with Windlow himself.

So for this last day she sat upon the tall horse as he fidgeted beneath her, sidling in and out of the shadows once more. "Be still, horse," she said, patting him without thinking. "We are waiting for a messenger."

The horse did not care. He had waited for three days and was not interested in waiting more. He jumped, hopped, shook his head violently until the links upon the bridle rang and jingled.

She dismounted with a sigh and led him upon the new grass of the hill. "Here then. Eat grass. Founder upon it. I'll not sit on your twitchiness longer."

She stretched her arms toward the threatening sky, shifting her ribs experimentally around the soreness remaining from the long ride east. She had left Battlefox Demesne last year, had spent the intervening seasons in Schlaizy Noithn—trying, without success, to remedy an unpleasantness in that tricksy land—and had come out not long ago to Shift into her own shape and equip herself for the journey. So, horse legs instead of her own legs; real clothing instead of mere Shifting; her own face instead of the grotesqueries she had used lately. There was nothing Shifty about her now, nothing to betray her except the quivering Shifter órgan deep within her which would announce the presence of another of her kind.

As it did now.

She crouched, ready to assume fangs and claws if needed for her own defense. There was no one on the road in either direction. She searched the dark forest from which a questioning howl rose, abruptly broken off, and her teeth lengthened slightly and her feet dug into the soil. The plump fustigar which trotted from the trees did not threaten her, however. It sat down a good distance from her, peered about itself with attention to the road and the surrounding thickets, then Shifted into a woman's shape clad much as Mavin was in tight breeches and boots.

"Mavin Manyshaped?" the woman said, beating the dust from her trousers. "I am Throsset of Dowes, and I come from the Seer Windlow."

Mavin's mouth dropped open. Throsset of Dowes? From Danderbat Keep? Mavin's own childhood home? Such as it had been. Well and well.

"Throsset of Dowes?" she asked wonderingly. "Would you remember Handbright of Danderbat Keep?"

The woman grinned. She was a stocky person with short, graying hair, bushy dark brows and eyes which protruded a little, giving her the look of a curious frog. Her shoulders were broad and square, and she shrugged them now, making an equivocal gesture. "Your sister, Handbright! Of course. She was younger than I. I tried to convince her to come with me, when I left the keep. She would not leave Danderbat the Old Shuffle."

"They said you were in love with a Demon, that you went across the seas with your lover."

The woman frowned, her face becoming suddenly distrustful. "The Danderbats said that, did they? Well, they'll say anything, those old ones. Likely Gormier said that. Or old Halfmad. Or others like them. I left, girl. So did you. It's likely we left for the same reasons, and lovers had no part in it."

"It was Handbright told me, not the old ones." Mavin felt an old anger, for Handbright, for herself.

"Ah." Throsset's voice turned cold, but her mouth looked tired. "She had to believe something, Mavin. She couldn't allow herself to believe that I simply *went*, that I got fed up with it and left. Girls of the Xhindi aren't supposed to do that, you know. We're supposed to be biddable—at least until we've had three or four childer to strengthen the keep. Well, it would be better to say the truth. I am not only Shifter, Mavin. When I was sixteen or so, one of the old ones tried something I didn't care for, and I found a new Talent. It seems I had Shifter and Sorcerer Talent both, and the Danderbats didn't know how to handle that. One Talent more and I'd have been a Dervish, and time was I longed for it, just to teach them a lesson. Still, there's no basket discipline will hold a wary Sorcerer, though they tried it, surely enough. I burst the basket and the room, and then I left. I'm sorry Handbright didn't go with me. How is she now?"

"Dead," said Mavin flatly, not caring to soften it.

"Dead!" The woman slapped at her legs, hands going on of themselves, without thought, as though they might brush the years away with the dust. "I hadn't heard. But then, I haven't been back to Danderbat Keep."

"They wouldn't have been able to tell you had you gone there. She died far away, across the western sea. She was mad —until the very end. She had two sons, twins. They're fifteen-season childer now, five years old, at Battlefox Demesne, with Handbright's thalan and mine, Plandybast Ogbone."

"So she did leave Danderbat at last. Ah, girl, believe me, I did try to get her to go with me. She said she stayed for your sake, and for Mertyn's. She loved him more than most sisters love their boy-kin. I could not break her loose."

Seeing the distress in the woman's face, Mavin tried to set aside her own remembered anger and to dissipate the chilliness which was growing between them. Handbright's servitude and abuse had not been Mavin's fault, or Throsset's. "Mertyn made her stay," she said sadly. "He had Beguilement Talent even then, and he used it to keep her there because he was afraid she would leave him. He was only a child. He did not know what pain it cost her. Well. That is all long gone, Throsset. Long gone. Done. Mertyn is a man now. Though his Talent was early, it has continued to grow. He is a King, I hear. Lately appointed Gamesmaster in some school or other."

"Windlow said to tell you he is in Schooltown." The woman stopped brushing dust and frowned. "Look, Mavin, I have traveled a distance and this is a high cold hill. There is threat of rain. I have not eaten today, and the city lies close below. . . ."

"We need not go so far as the city. There's an inn at the fork of the road, called The Arches. I have a room there." She lifted herself into the saddle. "Come up with me. This twitchy horse can carry double the short way." The woman grasped her arm and swung up behind her, the horse shying as he felt two sets of knees Shift tight around him. Deciding that obedience would be the most sensible thing, he turned quietly toward the road, going peaceably beneath each of the arches as he came to it with only a tiny twitch of skin along his flanks. The women rode in silence, both of them distressed at the meeting, for it raised old hurts and doubts to confront them.

It was not until they were seated before a small fire in a side room at the inn, cups of hot tea laced with wineghost half empty before them, that old sorrow gave way to new curiosity. Then they began to talk more freely, and Mavin found herself warming to the woman as she had not done to many others.

"How come you to be messenger for Windlow? A Shifter? He was Gamesmaster of the school at Tarnoch, under the protection of the High King. I would have thought he would send a Herald."

"I doubt he could have found a Herald to act for him. Windlow has little authority in the Demesne of the High King Prionde. Did you know the High King's son? Valdon?"

Mavin shuddered. Memories of that time—particularly of Valdon or Huld or Blourbast—still had the power to terrify her, if only for the moment. "I met him, yes. It was long ago.

He was little more than a boy. About nineteen? Full of vicious temper and arrogance. Yes. And his little brother, Boldery, who was a little older than Mertyn."

"Then if you met him it will not surprise you to know that Valdon refused to be schooled by Windlow. His pride would not allow him to be corrected, so says Windlow, and he could not bear restraint. He announced as much to the King, his father, and was allowed license to remain untaught."

Mavin had observed much of Valdon's prideful hostility when she had been in Pfarb Durim before. "But he wasn't the only student!" she objected. "Windlow had set up the school under the patronage of King Prionde, true, but there were many other boys involved. Some were thalans of most powerful Gamesmen."

"Exactly. You have hit upon the situation. Prionde could not destroy the school without hurting his own reputation. He could let it dwindle, however, and so he has done. Windlow is now alone in the school except for the servants and two or three boys, none of them of important families. Since Himaggery left, his only source of succor is through Boldery, for the child grew to love him and remains faithful, despite all Valdon's fulminations. Valdon is a Prince of easy hatreds and casual vengeance. A dangerous man."

Mavin twisted her mouth into a sceptical line. "Fellow Shifter, I sorrow to hear that the old man is not honored as he should be, and I am confirmed in my former opinion of Valdon, but Windlow has not sent you all this way from the high lakes at Tarnoch to tell me of such things."

Throsset gulped a mouthful of cooling tea and shook her head. "Of course not. I owed the old man many things. He asked me to come to you as a favor, because I am Shifter from Danderbat Keep, and you are Shifter from Danderbat Keep, and he believed you would trust my word. . . ."

"Trust you because we are both from Danderbat Keep!" Mavin could not keep the astonishment from her voice.

Throsset made a grimace. "Unless you told him, what would he know about the lack of trust and affection in Danderbat Keep? That wasn't what he was thinking of, in any case. He asked me because we were both women there. That old man understands much, Mavin. I think you may have told him more about yourself than you realized, and I certainly told him more than I have told anyone else. He senses things, too. Things that most Gamesmen simply ignore. No, Windlow didn't send me to tell you of his own misfortune. He sent me to bring to you everything he knows about Himaggery—where he went, where he might be."

"But he is dead!" Mavin cried, her voice breaking.

"Hush your shouting," commanded Throsset in a hissing whisper. "It is your business, perhaps our business, but not the business of the innkeeper and every traveler on the road. He is not dead. Windlow says no!"

"Not dead? And yet gone for eight years, and I only hear of it now!"

"Of course now. How could you have heard of it earlier? Did Windlow know where you were? Did you send regular messengers to inform him?" Throsset was good-natured but scornful. "Of course, now."

"He is a Seer," Mavin said sullenly, aware of her lack of logic.

"Poof. Seers. Sometimes they know everything about something no one cares about. Often they know nothing about something important. Windlow himself says that. He knows where Himaggery set out to go eight years ago; he Sees very little about where he may be now."

"Eight years!"

"It seems a long time to me, too."

"Eight years. Eight years ago—I was . . . where was I?" She fell silent, thinking, then flushed a brilliant red which went unnoticed in the rosy firelight. Eight years ago she had wandered near the shadowmarches, had found herself in a pool-laced forest so perfect that it had summoned her to take a certain shape within it, the shape of a slender, single-horned beast with golden hooves. And then there had been another of the same kind, a male. And they two . . . they two . . . Ah. It was only a romantic, erotic memory, an experience so glorious that she had refused to have any other such for fear it would fail in comparison. Whenever she remembered it, she grieved anew at the loss, and even now she grieved to remember what had been then and was no more. She shook her head, tried to clear it, to think only of this new hope that perhaps Himaggery still lived. "Eight years. Where did he set out for, that long ago?"

"He set out to meet with the High Wizard Chamferton."

"I know that much; his letter said that much. But why? Himaggery was Wizard himself. Why would he seek another?"

Throsset rose to sidle through the narrow door into the commons room of the inn where she ordered another pot of tea. She came into the room carrying a second flask of wine-ghost, peeling at the wax on the cork with her teeth. "Two more cups of this and I'll be past the need for food and fit only for bed. Don't you ever get hungry?"

Mavin made an irritated gesture. It was no time to think of food, but her stomach gurgled in that instant, brought to full attention by Throsset's words. The woman laughed. When the boy came in with the tea, Throsset ordered food to be prepared, then settled before the fire once more.

"You asked why he sought another Wizard. I asked the same question of Windlow. He told me a tale of old Monuments that danced, of ancient things which stir and rumble at the edges of the lands of the True Game. He told me of a time, perhaps sixty years ago or so, when great destruction was wrought upon the lands, and he said it was not the first time. He had very ancient books which spoke of another time, so long ago it is past all memory, when people were driven from one place to another, when the beasts of this world assembled against them. He spoke of roads and towers and bells, of shadows and rolling stars. Mysteries, he said, which intrigued Himaggery and sent him seeking. Old Chamferton was said to know something about these ancient mysteries."

Mavin tilted her head, considering this. "I have heard of at least one such time," she said. "Across the seas there is a land which suffered such a cataclysm a thousand years ago. The people were driven down into a great chasm by beasts which came suddenly, from nowhere."

"Stories of that kind fascinated Himaggery," Throsset mused, "as they do me. Oh, we heard them as children, Mavin! Talking animals and magical rings. Swords and jewels and enchanted maidens. Himaggery collected such tales, says Windlow. He traveled all about the countryside staying in old inns, asking old pawnish granddads what stories they remembered from the time before our ancestors came from the north."

"You say our ancestors came from the north? In Schlaizy Noithn I have heard it rumored we came from beneath the mountains! And across the seas, in the chasm of which I spoke earlier, the priests say the Boundless—that being their name for their god—set them in their chasm."

Throsset turned up her hands, broadening the gesture to embrace the space near the table as the boy came into the room with their food. "Ah. Set it here, boy, and bring another dish of that sauce. This isn't enough for two! Good. Smell that, Mavin? Cookery like this always reminds me of Assembly time at Danderbat Keep."

Mavin did not want to remember Assembly time at Danderbat Keep. "The food was the best part of it," she remarked in a dry tone of recollection.

"It was that," Throsset agreed around a mouthful. "But we have enough sad memories between us without dragging them out into the light. They do not grow in the dark, I think, so much as they do when well aired and fertilized with tears."

Mavin agreed. "Very well, Kinswoman, I will not dwell on old troubles. We are here now, not at the Keep, and it is here we will think of. Now, you tell me Himaggery had heard all these tales of ancient things. I can tell you, for you are in Windlow's confidence, that Himaggery himself saw those arches dance, those Monuments where we met today; and so did I—Yes! If you could see your face, Throsset. You obviously disbelieve me. You don't trust my account for a moment, but it's true nonetheless. Some future time, I'll tell you all about it if you like— Well, I saw the arches dance, but afterward I was willing to leave it at that, perhaps to remember it from time to time, but not to tease at it and tear at it. Not Himaggery! Himaggery had a mind full of little tentacles and claws, reaching, always reaching. He was never willing to leave anything alone until he understood it.

"Strange are the Talents of Wizards, so it's said, and strange are the ways they think. Once he had seen, he couldn't have left it alone, not for a moment. He'd have been after it like a gobble-mole with a worm, holding on, stretching it out longer and longer until it popped out of its hole. And if he heard the High Wizard Chamferton knew anything—well then, off he'd go, I suppose." She felt uneasy tears welling up.

Throsset confirmed this. "Yes, he heard it said that Chamferton knew about the mysteries of our past and the past of the world and ancient things in general. So. He went off to see Chamferton, and he did not come back."

"But Windlow knows he is not dead?"

"Windlow knows Himaggery lives."

"Not mere wishful thinking?" Mavin turned away from the firelight and rubbed her eyes, suddenly a little hopeful, yet still hesitant to accept it. "Windlow must be getting very old."

"About eighty-five, I should say. He is remarkably active still. No. He says that Gamesmen, often the finest and the best of them, do disappear from time to time into a kind of nothingness from which the Necromancers cannot raise them, into an oblivion, leaving no trace. But Himaggery's disappearance is not of that kind."

"How does he know?"

"For many years, Windlow has been collecting old books. He sends finders out to locate them and get them by beggery, barter, or theft, so he says. During the last several years he has asked these finders to search for Himaggery also. Some of them returned to say they felt Himaggery's presence, have sought and sought, felt it still, but were unable to find him. And this is not old information; a Rancelman came back with some such tale only a few days before I left there."

"So Windlow has sent you to tell me Himaggery is not dead but vanished and none of the Pursuivants or Rancelmen can find him." Mavin said this flatly as she wiped sauce from her chin, keeping both her voice and her body still and unresponsive. The tears were in abeyance for the moment, and she would not acknowledge them. It would do no good to weep over her food while Throsset chewed and swallowed and cast curious glances at her over the edge of her cup. It would do no good until she could think of something else to do besides weeping. Despite her hunger, the food lay inside her like stone.

She pushed the plate away, suddenly nauseated. The firelight made a liquid swimming at the corners of her eyes.

"Tush," mourned Throsset. "You're not enjoying your dinner at all. Cry if you like! We don't make solemn vows over twenty years unless there is something to it besides moon madness. Was he your lover?"

She shook her head, tears spilling down her face in an unheeded flood, dripping from her chin onto her clenched hands. Her throat closed as in a vice, almost as it had done when she had read his letter.

Throsset got up and closed the door, leaning a chair against it. Then she walked around the room, saying nothing, while Mavin brought herself to a gulping silence. When that time came, she brought a towel and dipped it into the pitcher on the table. "Here. Wash the tears away before they begin to itch. You have a puddle on your breeches. They'll think you've wet yourself. Come to the fire and dry it. Now, you don't need any more wineghost, that's certain. It won't cure tears. Take some of the tea for your throat. You'll have cried yourself hoarse. . . ."

After a time, Mavin could speak again. "I am not much of a weeper, Throsset. I have not wept for many years, even when I have made others weep. I don't really know why I'm doing it now. No, Himaggery and I weren't lovers. We could have been. I was very much . . . desirous of him. But I kept him from it, kept me from it. I did not want that, not then. There was too much of servitude in it, too much of Danderbat Keep."

The woman nodded. "Anyone who grew up in Danderbat Keep would understand that. Still, there was something between you, whether you let anything actually happen or not." She took the towel and wrung it out before handing it to Mavin once more. "Windlow told me of some joke between you and Himaggery. That Himaggery was not his true name at all, that you had made up the name."

"Mertyn and I made it up on our trip north from Danderbat Keep. To avoid being bothered by child stealers and pawners, I was to say that I was the servant of the Wizard Himaggery—which was a name we invented—and that he, Mertyn, was thalan to the Wizard. In this way, we hoped to avoid trouble or Gaming as we traveled north. For a time it worked. Then we were accused of lying—accused by Huld." She shivered, remembering the malevolence in that Demon's voice and manner.

"And then this casual young man came into the room saying the accusation was nonsense; that he was himself the Wizard Himaggery and that I, Mavin, was indeed his servant. And so the threat passed. Afterward, he said he would keep the name. I thought at the time it suited him better than his own."

"And that was all that passed between you?"

"That. And a night together on a hillside among the shadowpeople. And a few hours in Pfarb Durim at the hotel Mudgery Mont when the plague and the battle and the crisis were all over. And a promise."

"And yet you wept. . . ."

"And yet I wept. Perhaps the weeping was for many things. For Handbright, because you knew her. And for the young Throsset of Dowes as well. For old Windlow, perhaps, who has not received the honors he deserves. And for me and the eight years I have wandered the world not knowing Himaggery was gone. I had imagined him, you know, many times, as he would look when I met him again at last. I saw his face, clearly as in a mirror. It is almost as though I had known him during these years, been with him. When I rode to Pfarb Durim, I knew how familiar he would look to me, even after all this time. . . ." She wiped her face one final time, then folded the towel and placed it on the table near her half-emptied plate. "Well. I am wept out now. And I know there must be more to this than you have told me. Windlow could have put this in the same letter he sent to Mudgery Mont."

"He could," agreed Throsset, piling the dishes to one side before returning to her cup. "He could. Yes. He did not, for various reasons. First, there are always those who read letters who have no business reading them. Particularly in Pfarb Durim. Huld still has great influence there, I understand, and every second person in the city is involved in gathering information for him."

"That's true. Though I was told at Mudgery Mont that Huld repented of Blourbast's reputation and will stay in Bannerwell from now on."

"No matter where he stays, spies who work for him will still sneak a look at other people's letters. In addition, however, there are those abroad in the world who have no love for Himaggery. I speak now of Valdon. Windlow did not tell me the source of the enmity. Perhaps he does not even know. But Windlow would put nothing in writing which might be used to harm him.

"In any case, that was not the main reason Windlow sent me. He says he had a vision, years ago, when you were all here before, in which he saw you and Himaggery together in Pfarb Durim. Somehow in the vision he knew that twenty years had passed. So, says Windlow, if Himaggery is to come here again and the vision to be fulfilled, then you, Mavin, must be involved in it."

"He wants me to go searching, does he?"

"He thinks you will. He never said what he wanted."

Mavin made a rather sour smile, thinking of the leagues she had traveled since her girlhood. "I spent fifteen years searching for Handbright, did you know that? No, of course you didn't. I could have done it in less time. I might have saved her life if I had been quicker. When that search was done, I was glad it was over. I am not a Pursuivant who takes pleasure in the chase, Throsset. My experience is that searching is weary work. I don't know what I will do, Kinswoman. As you say, we were not lovers."

"Still, you made a promise."

"To meet him here. Not to find him and bring him here."

"Still, a promise . . . well. It is no part of my duty to chivvy you one way or the other. Only you know what passed between the two of you long ago and whether it was enough to send you on this journey. Only you know why you have been crying as though your heart would break. I have done as I promised the old Seer I would do—brought you word. No. I have not done entirely. He sent a map of the lands where the High Wizard Chamferton dwells, if indeed he dwells there still. It is a copy of the one Himaggery took with him. It is here on the table."

"Are you leaving? So soon?"

"No. I am taking a room in this place for the night, unless you will let me share yours. Whichever, I will go there now to sleep. Which you should do, unless you are determined to linger by the fire and think deep thoughts. If I thought I could help you, I would offer to do so, for long ago I cared about Handbright. Cared for her, failed her. There should have been something more I could have done, but at the time I thought I had done everything." She stared into the fire herself, obviously thinking deep thoughts of her own.

Mavin, curious, asked, "Is there a name for this combination of Talents you have, Trosset? I have gone over and over what little I know of the Index, and I cannot remember what Gamesname you should be called."

Throsset flushed. "There is a name, Mavin. I would prefer to be called simply Shifter, if you must call me. Or Sorcerer, if Shifter is not enough. I sometimes think those anonymous ancestors who made up the Index suffered from an excess of humor. Their name for one of my Talents is not one I choose to bear. Well. No matter what I might have called myself, Handbright would not hear me when I spoke to her. You have not said how it was she left at last."

Mavin murmured a few words about the lateness of the hour, indicating she did not want to talk about it then. The thought of Handbright saddened her always, and she was sad enough at the moment over other things. Throsset nodded in return, signifying that another time would do. The time did not come, however. When Mavin woke in the morning, the bed beside her was empty and Throsset was gone. The map lay on a chest beside the door. The innkeeper said the account had been paid.

Outside in the stableyard Mavin's tall horse whickered, and after a time of thought Mavin sold him to the innkeeper. Somehow in the deep night the matter had become decided, and she needed no flesh but her own to carry her to whatever place Himaggery had gone.

Chapter 2

There was a note attached to the map with a silver pin. "Mavin, my dear child, this is a copy of the map Himaggery and I made up before he left. Most of the information is from some old books I had, but we got one or two things from some recent charts made by Yggery, the Mapmaker in Xammer. Himaggery was to go first to Chamferton, who is reputed to have access to an old library. If you decide to go looking for Himaggery, there is no point in coming here. Everything I know is on the map or Throsset will have told you. I hope you will want to go after him. I would do so if these aging legs would carry me, for he is very dear to me." It was signed with Windlow's seal, and she stood staring at it for a very long time.

She bought a few provisions from the Arches, more for appearance's sake than anything else. It was better to let those who saw her upon the road, those who might speak of her to others, think she had had to sell the horse to buy food than that they know her for a Shifter who could live off the countryside as well as any pombi or fustigar. Shifters were not highly regarded in the world of the True Game, not by Gamesmen or pawns, and there was recurrent unpleasantness to remind her of it. Better to be merely another anonymous person and wait until she was out of sight of the inn before Shifting into a long-legged form in which she could run all day without weariness—in which she had run day after day in Schlaizy Noithn.

According to the map, the High Wizard Chamferton dwelt in the Dorbor Range, east of the shadowmarches, in a long canyon which led from the cliffs above the Lake of Faces northward among the mountains. Mavin knew her way to the shadowmarches well enough. She had traveled there before; to Battlefox the Bright Day, where her own kin lived in a Shifters' demesne; to the lands of the shadowpeople where Proom lived with his tribe, wide-eared and bright-fanged, singing their way through the wide world and laughing at everything; to Ganver's Grave, the place of the Eesties, or Eestnies as some called them; to that enchanted, pool-laced valley she remembered in her dreams where the two fabulous beasts had lain together in beds of fragrant moss. North. The location did not surprise her. If she had been told to seek out knowledge of ancient things, northward is the way she would have gone. Still, the paths she knew would not help her in coming to Chamferton. She had not been that route before.

Bidding a polite farewell to the innkeeper she stepped onto the road and walked northward on it. The night's storm had given way to a morning of pale wet light and steamy green herbage dotted with flowers. Far to the west she could see Cagihiggy Creek in a blaze of webwillow, yellow as morning. It was calming to walk, stride on stride, aware of the day without worrying where night would find her. She yawned widely as she turned aside from the road onto the wooded slope of the hills.

She was now a little east of Pfarb Durim, ready to run in fustigar shape along these eastern hills until she came some distance north of Hell's Maw. Having walked into that labyrinth once, she had no desire to see it or smell it again. Once she was far enough north, she would climb down the cliff in order to reach the Lake of the Faces, a new feature upon the maps, created, so it was said, only within recent years. She had a mind to see it, to learn if what was said of it was true, though half her mind mocked the rest of her with believing such wild tales. Still, there would be no time wasted.

The Lake of Faces lay in the valley below the entrance to the canyon where the Demesne of the High Wizard Chamferton would be found. She felt the map, tightly folded in her pocket. Once she abandoned her clothing, she would make a pocket in her hide for it.

Soon she was lost among the trees, invisible to any eyes except small wild ones peering from high branches or hidey holes among the roots. Keeping only the little leather bag which held her supply of coin, she put her clothing into a hollow tree, the boots dropping against the trunk with a satisfying clunk. Fur crept over her limbs, sensuously, slowly, so she could feel the tickling emergence of it; bones flexed and bent into new configurations. She dropped to all fours, set eyes and nose to see and hear the world in a way her own form could never do. A bunwit flashed away among the bushes, frightened out of its few wits by this sudden appearance of a fustigar. Mavin licked her nose with a wet tongue and loped away to the north. A bunwit like that one would make her supper, and she would not necessarily feel the need to cook it.

Dark came early, but she did not stop until she had reached the edge of the cliff and crawled down it in a spidery bundle of legs and claws. Once at the bottom she could smell water and hear many trickling falls, thin and musical in the dark. A shaving of moon lit the Lake of Faces and made silver streamers of the water dropping into it from the cliffs above. The spider shape yawned, Shifted; the fustigar yawned, Shifted. Mavin stood in her own shape upon the shore, ivory in the cool night. She scratched. Whatever shape one Shifted into, the skin stayed on the outside and all the dirt of the road stayed on it. The water welcomed her as she slid beneath its surface, relishing its chill caress.

The lake had been so inviting she had taken no time to look around her. Now, floating on her back with her hair streaming below her like black water weed in the moonlight, she began to see the Faces.

White poles emerged from shadow as she peered into the dark, an army of them in scattered battalions on the shore, in the shallows, marching out into the fringes of the forest. One such stood close beside her, and she clung to it, measuring it with hands which would not quite reach around it, finger to finger, thumb to thumb. She lay on the water and thrust herself away from the pole so she could look up into the face at its top, white as ivory, blind-eyed, close-lipped, its scalp resting upon the top of the pole, a thin strap extending from ear to ear behind the pole and nailed there with a silver spike.

It was a woman's face, a mature woman, not thin, not lovely but handsome. The face had no hair, only the smooth curve as of a shaved skull, pale as bleached bone.

Though it seemed no more alive than a statue and was no more real, it troubled her. She swam away a little, found another of the white posts and confronted a man's face, weak-jawed and petulant-looking, the blind eyes gleaming with reflected light. The moon had come higher, making the pale poles stand out against the dark of the forested cliffs like a regiment of ghosts.

From high above the cliffs, a scream shattered the silence; the harsh, predatory cry of some huge bird. Mavin looked up to see two winged blots circling down toward the lake. Shifting herself, she sank beneath the waters to peer at them with protruding, froglike eyes.

Harpies! She edged upward, let her ears rest above the water in the shadow of the pole, drawn by something familiar in the cry. Yes. Though she had not heard that voice for twenty years, she could not mistake it. One of the descending forms was Pantiquod—Pantiquod who had brought the plague to Pfarb Durim, who had almost killed Mertyn, who should have been far to the south at Bannerwell with her evil children—screaming a welcome to another child.

"Well met, daughter! I thought to find you during new moon at the Lake of Faces. And here you are, at old Chamferton's oracle. Does he send you still to question the Faces?"

The voice in reply was as harsh, as metallic, with an undertone of wild laughter in it. "Pantiquod, mother-bird, I had begun to think you too old to take shape. What brings you?" The two settled upon the shore, folding their wings to stalk about on high, stork legs, bare pendulous breasts gleaming in the moonlight. Mavin became aware of a smell, a poultry house stink, chemical and acrid. Shifting her eyes to gather more light, she saw that the shore among the poles was littered with Harpy droppings, white as the masks themselves.

"Not too old, daughter. Too lazy, perhaps. Since Blourbast is dead, I have luxuriated with no need to Game or bestir myself."

"And how are my half sister and brother," the younger Harpy cried, voice dripping venom. "The lovely Huldra, the lovelier Huld?"

"Well enough, daughter. Well enough. Since Huldra bore a son, Mandor, she has had little to do with Huld. She hates him, and he her, and both me and I both. I do not let it trouble me. I stay with them for the power and the servants and the comfort. In the caves beneath Bannerwell there is much pleasure to be had."

"I can imagine. Years of such pleasure you've had already. More years than I can remember, yet never a word from you since Blourbast died. Why now, mama? Why now, loathsome chicken?" And she cawed with wild laughter, at some joke which Pantiquod shared, for the older Harpy shrilled in the same tone.

"Oh, does Chamferton call you that still? And me as well? I came not before, dear daughter, because I do not serve him still and would not be caught again in his toils. I come now because you do serve him still and I want to borrow *it* from you. For a moment or two."

"I do not serve him. He holds me, as he once held us both. And you want to borrow it? The wand? Foolishness, mother-bird. He would know it in a minute."

"Would it matter if he did? After eight long years, is he still so violent? Would he punish you? For granting a small request to your own mother?"

The younger Harpy lifted on her wings, threw her head back and screamed with laughter, jigged on her stork legs, wings out, dancing. "Would Chamferton punish me? Would Chamferton punish me? What a question, a question!"

Mavin paddled her way closer to the shore. They were talking more quietly now, the screaming greetings done, and she thrust her ears upward to catch each word.

"I will not lend it to you, Mother. Do not ask it. Try to take it and I'll claw your gizzard out and your eyes as well. But I'll use it for you, perhaps, if you have not any purpose in mind Chamferton would find hateful enough to punish me for."

"It is no purpose he would care a thrilpskin for. Does he care for Huld? Is the Face of Huld still here?"

"He cares nothing for Huld, and the Face is still here, where he had you put it, Mother. Long ago."

"He has probably forgotten it. But I have not forgotten, and I need to know from it a little thing. Ask it for me: Will it grow and flourish like webwillow in the spring? Or will it shrivel and die? Ask it for me, daughter. And I will then do then what is best . . . for me."

The two stork-legged shapes moved away among the poles, Mavin after them flat as a shadow on the ground, invisible as she crept in their wake. They wound their way through the forest of poles, searching for a particular one. At last they found it, cawing to one another excitedly. "Oh, it is Huld's Face, as he is today. He was handsomer when young, daughter. For a time I thought him a very marvel of beauty, before Blourbast changed him and made him what he is."

"Ahh, cahhh, ah-haa, mate a Ghoul with a Harpy and blame the Ghoul's influence for what comes out. Well, Mother. Shall I ask?"

There were whispers. Then the younger Harpy stood back from the pole with its Face and called strange words into the silence of the place, striking the pole three times with a long, slender wand she had drawn from a case on her back. Three times she repeated this invocation. On the ninth blow, the lips of the Face opened and Huld's voice spoke—Huld's voice as it would have come from another world, beyond space. It was the timeless ghost of his voice, and it made shivers where Mavin's backbones might have been.

"What would you know?"

"Will you live or die, Huld?" asked the Harpy. "Will you flourish or wilt into nothing?"

"For a season I will flourish. I will lose that which I now hold precious and discover I care not. I will heap atrocity upon atrocity to build a name and will lose even my name in a dust of bones." The lips of the Face snapped shut with the sound of stones striking together. The young Harpy spun on her tall legs, snickering.

"So, Mother? Is that enough?"

"It is enough," Pantiquod said in a dry, harsh voice. "I felt something of the kind. A pity. If one would choose, one would choose a son who would not be so ephemeral. Still. It is he who will dwindle and die, not I. There is time for me to protect myself. I will be leaving Bannerwell, daughter."

"And your other daughter, lovely Huldra?"

"As she will. She may choose to stay, or go."

"Where will you go?"

"If I do not wish to share Huld's eventual ruin, away from him. Into the Northlands, I think. I have heard there are fortunes to be made and damage to be done in the Northlands. And I will not go empty-handed."

"Ah-haw, cawh, I would think not. Will you wait with me now, Mother, while I do Chamferton's bidding? Will you keep me company?"

"We were never company, daughter," said Pantiquod, rising on her wings and making a cloud of dry, feathery droppings scud across the ground into Mavin's face. "But I fly now to Chamferton's aerie, and you may return there before I go. Maybe he will have news for me of doings in the north." She flew up, circling, crying once at the top of the spiral before wheeling north along the valley.

Now the younger Harpy moved among the Faces, chattering to herself like a barnyard fowl, full of clucks and keraws. Three times she stopped before Faces and demanded certain information of them. Three times the Faces replied before returning to their silent, expressionless masks. A man with a young-old Face was asked where he was and answered, "Under Bartelmy's Ban." It was a strange Face and a strange answer. Both stuck in Mavin's memory. An old woman's Face opened its pale lips and chanted, "Upon the road, the old road, a tower made of stone. In the tower hangs a bell which cannot ring alone. . . ." There was a long pause, then the lips opened once more. "The daylight bell still hangs in the last tower." The Harpy chuckled at this before going on to the next face, that of a middle-aged man with a missing eye who announced that the Great Game being played in the midlands near Lake Yost would soon be lost for all who played, with only death as a result and the Demesne of Lake Yost left vacant.

By the time Mavin had heard the words of invocation said

three times for each of these, she could have quoted them herself. The moon was high above. The young Harpy seemed to have finished her assigned duties and now moved among the poles and Faces only for amusement, Mavin still following doggedly, her curiosity keeping her close behind.

She almost missed seeing Himaggery's face, her eyes sliding across it as they had a hundred others, only to return, shocked and fascinated. It was the face of a man in his mid years, perhaps forty, with lines from nose to mouth and a web around his eyes. And yet—and yet see how those lips quirked in a way she had remembered always, and the lines around his eyes were those her fingertips remembered. He looked as she had dreamed he would, as she had known he would, and that second look told her it was he beyond all doubt.

She came up from the guano-smeared soil in one unthinking movement, grasping the Harpy with fingers of steel before she could react.

"I will take the wand, daughter of Pantiquod."

The Harpy did not reply, but began a wild, wheeling struggle, beating her wings against Mavin's face, thrusting with her strong talons. When she found she could not escape, she began screaming, raising echoes which fled along the lake-shore, rousing birds who nested there so that they, too, screamed in the night. Mavin felt the distant beating of wings, heard a cry from high above, knew that fliers there could plunge upon her in moments.

"Call them off," she instructed breathlessly. "At once. I have no desire to kill you, Harpy, unless I must."

There was only a defiant caw of rage as the Harpy re-doubled her struggles. Mavin shook her, snapped her like a whip, raised her above to serve as a shield—and felt the talons and beak of whatever had plummeted from the sky bury them-selves in the Harpy's body. Abruptly the struggles ceased.

Mavin dropped the body. Perched upon it was a stunned flitchhawk, its dazed, yellow eyes opaque. Mavin pulled it from the Harpy's throat and tossed it away. It planed down onto the soil to crouch there, panting.

Mavin turned her back on the bird. She drew the Harpy's wand from its case. The battle had driven the words of invoca-tion from her memory, and it took a moment to recall them.

Then she stood before Himaggery's Face and chanted them, striking with the wand three times, three times again, and a final three.

The stony lips opened. "What would you know?" asked the ghost of Himaggery's voice.

"Where are you?" she begged. "Where are you, Himaggery?"

"Under the Ban, the Ban, Bartelmy's Ban," said the ghostly voice, and the lips shut tight.

She had heard that meaningless answer before! She tried to open his lips again with the wand and the words, but it did no good. She wandered among the Faces, to see if there were others she knew. There were none. At length her weariness overtook her, and she returned to the water to wash away the harsh, biting smell of the place. After that was a long time of sleep on a moss bank, halfway up the cliff, where no Harpies had come to leave their droppings. And long after that, morning which was more than halfway to noon.

She went down to the lake for water. The Harpy lay where Mavin had thrown her the night before, dried blood upon her throat and chest. That chest moved, however, in slow breaths, and the wound had clotted over. Mavin mused at this for some time before turning to the water. When she had washed herself and found something juicy for her breakfast, she returned to the Harpy's unconscious form and took it upon her back. "I will return you to your master," she announced in a cheery tone, Shifting to spider legs which could carry them both up the precipitous cliffs around the lake. "You and your wand—the Wizard's wand. It may be he will be grateful."

"And if he is not?" asked some inner sceptical part of her. "And if Pantiquod is there?"

"Well then, not," she answered, still cheerily. "He can do no worse than try to enchant me, or whatever it is Wizards do. I can do no better than Shift into something horrible and eat him if he tries it. So and so. As for Pantiquod . . . likely she will have gone on by now. She did not intend to await her daughter's coming."

The spider shape gave way to her lean, fustigar form when she reached the cliff top. Before her the canyon stretched away in long diagonals where the toes of two mountains touched, northwest then northeast then northwest once more. The small river in its bottom was no more than a sizeable creek, bright shallow water sparkling over brown stones and drifts of gravel. Fish fled from the shallows where she stood and something jumped into the water upstream, bringing ripples to her feet.

She lapped at the water, feeling it cool upon her furry legs. The water joined her breakfast to add bulk, making the body on her back less burdensome. Squirming to get it more comfortably settled, she trotted up the canyon into the trees, which grew thicker the farther north she went.

At noon she put her burden down, caught two ground-running birds, Shifted into her own form and cooked them above a small fire as she watched the smoke, smelled it, smiled and hummed. The mood of contentment was rare and inexplicable. She knew she should feel far otherwise, but as the day wore on, the calm and content continued to grow.

"Enchantment!" her inner self warned. "This is enchantment, Mavin."

"So," she purred to herself. "Let be. What will come will come."

It was dusk when she rounded a last curve of the canyon to see the fortress before her, its battlements made of the same stone it stood upon, gray and ancient, as though formed in the cataclysm which had reared the mountains up. There was a flash of light from the tower, like a mirror reflecting sun from the craggy horizon. In that instant, the mood of contentment lifted, leaving behind a feeling of dazed weariness, as when one had drunk too much and caroused too late. She knew someone had seen her, had weighed her up and determined that the protection of enchantment was not necessary any longer. She snarled to herself, accepting it.

After waiting a few moments to see whether anything else would happen, she trotted forward. A road began just before her, winding, grown over in places, but a road nonetheless. She followed it, tongue out and panting. The way had been long and mostly uphill. Breakfast and lunch were long gone.

The fortress stood very high upon its sheer plinth of stone. From the canyon floor, stairs wound into darkness up behind the pillar. Mavin dropped her burden and lay down at the foot of these stairs, first nosing the Harpy to determine whether she still lived. She stretched, rolled, then began licking sore paws. She would stay as she was, thank you, until something definitive happened. She was not about to get caught in any shape at all on that dark, ominous staircase.

"Is that as far as you intend to bring her?" asked a hoarse, contentious voice from the stairs.

She looked up. He stood there, framed against the dark, in all respects a paradigm of Wizards. He had the cloak and robe, the tall hat, the beard, the crooked nose and the stern mouth. She was silent, expecting sparks to fly from his fingers. None did. He seemed content to stand there and wait.

Mavin fidgeted. Well. And why not? She Shifted, coming up from the fustigar shape into her own, decently clothed, with a Shifted cloak at her shoulders. Let the man know she was no savage.

"I had need to borrow her wand," said Mavin flatly. "She fought me."

"So you wounded her. Considerably, from the look of her."

"She called down a flitchhawk from the sky. It wounded her. I thought her dead until this morning. Then, when I saw she breathed, I decided to return her to you."

"What did you expect me to do with her in that state?" There was a movement behind the Wizard as someone emerged upon the stair, a tall, gray woman in a feathered headdress—no longer in Harpy's shape. Pantiquod.

Mavin shrugged elaborately, pretending not to see her. "If she has value, I presume you will have her Healed. If she has none, then it doesn't matter what you do. In any case, I have returned your property. All of it." She took the wand from her shoulder and laid it upon the Harpy's breast where it moved slowly up and down with her breathing.

Pantiquod screamed! She started down the stairs, pouring out threats in that same colorless voice Mavin had heard her use in Pfarb Durim, hands extended like claws, aimed for Mavin's throat. "Shifter bitch! It was you killed Blourbast! You who set our plans awry! You who have wounded my daughter, my Foulitter. Bitch, I'll have your eyes. . . ."

The Wizard gestured violently at the Harpy, crying some strange words in a loud voice, and the woman stopped as though she had run into a wall. "Back," the Wizard shouted. "Back to your perch in the mews, loathsome chicken. Back before I put an end to you." The woman turned and moved away, reluctantly, and not before casting Mavin one last, hissing threat. Mavin shivered, trying not to let it show.

Somewhere nearby a door banged. There were clattering footsteps, and several forms erupted from the dark stairway. Servitors. The Wizard pointed to the limp body.

"Take her to the mews. Maldin, see if the Healer is in her rooms. If not, then find her. Fermin, take that wand up to the tower and hang it on the back of the door where it belongs." He turned to Mavin and gestured toward the stairs. "Well, Shifter, you had best come in. Since you have taken the trouble to return my property, it seems only fitting to offer some thanks, and some apologies for a certain one of my servants."

Mavin stared upward. The castle loomed high above her, an endless stair length. She sighed.

He interpreted her weariness correctly. "Oh, we won't climb up there. No, no. We use that fortification only when we must. When Game is announced, you know, and it's the only appropriate place. It's far too lofty to be useful for ordinary living. Besides, it's impossible to heat." He turned to one of the servants who still lurked in the shadowy stair. "Jowret, tell the kitchen there'll be a guest for supper. Tell them to serve us in my sitting room. Now, just up one flight, young woman, and through the door where you see the light. To your left, please. Ah, now just open that door before you. And here we are. Fire, wine, even a bit of cheese if hunger nibbles at you this early."

He took off his tall hat and sat in a comfortable-appearing chair before the tiled stove, motioning her to a similar one across the table; and he stared at her from under his brows, trying not to let her see that he did so.

Uncomfortably aware of this scrutiny, Mavin cut a piece of cheese and sat down to eat it, examining him no less covertly.

Without the tall hat he was less imposing. Though there were heavy brows over his brooding eyes, the eyes themselves were surrounded with puffy, unhealthy-looking flesh, as though he slept too little or drank too much. When she had swallowed, she said, "I overheard the two Harpies talking. I know Pantiquod from a former time, from the place they call Hell's Maw. She called the other her daughter."

"I doubt they spoke kindly of me," he said sneeringly, reaching for the cheese knife. "Both of them attempted to do me an injury some years ago. I put them under durance until the account is paid. Pantiquod was sly enough to offer me some recompense, so I freed her, in a manner of speaking. The daughter was the worse of the two. She owes me servitude for yet a few years."

"She questioned the Faces. I heard her doing it. Three of them for you. One for Pantiquod." Mavin hesitated for a moment, doubting whether it would be wise to say more. However, if she were to find any trace of Himaggery, some risk was necessary. "And then I took the wand away from her and questioned one myself."

"Someone you know?" His voice was like iron striking an anvil.

"Someone I'm looking for. He set out eight years ago to find you. His friends have not seen him since."

"Oh," he said, darting one close, searching look at her before shrugging with elaborate nonchalance. "That would be the Wizard Himaggery, I think. He stopped here, bringing two old dames with him from Betand. Foolish." He did not explain this cryptic utterance, and Mavin did not interrupt to ask him to clarify it. "He'd been collecting old tales, songs, rhymes. Wanted to solve some of the ancient mysteries. Well. What are Wizards for if not to do things like that? Hmmm? He wanted to go north. I told him it was risky, even foolish. He was young—barely thirty? Thirty-two? Hardly more than a youth." He shook his head. "Well, so you found his Face." He seemed to await some response to this, almost holding his breath. Mavin could sense his caution and wondered at it.

"You put it there?" She kept her voice casual. There was a strange tickle in her head, as though the man before her sought to Read her mind. Or perhaps some other person hidden nearby. She had never heard that Wizards had that Talent.

"Well, yes. I put it there. It does them little damage. Scarcely a pinprick."

"How did you do that? What for?" Still that probing tickle.

"How do I make the Faces?" He leaned back, evidently re-assured that she carried the question of Himaggery's Face no further. "It would take several years to explain. You said your name was? Ah. Mavin. Well, Mavin, it would take a long time to explain. It took me several decades to learn to do it. Suffice it to say that the Lake is located at some kind of—oh, call it a nexus. A time nexus. If one takes a very thin slice of person and faces it forward, just at that nexus, then the slice can see into its future. That is, the person's future. Some of them can see their own end, some only a little way into tomorrow. And if one commands a Face to tell—using the right gramarye, a wand properly prepared and so forth—then it tells what it sees. Believe me, I use only a very thin slice. The donors never miss it." Again he seemed to be waiting some response from her.

Why should he care whether I believe him or not, she thought. This question seemed too dangerous to ask. She sub-stituted another. "Why did you want to know his future?"

He paused before answering, and Mavin seemed to hear a warning vibration in her mind, a hissing, a rattle, as when something deadly is disturbed. She leaned forward to cut another piece of cheese, acting her unconcern. This misdirec-tion seemed to quiet him, for the strange mental feeling passed as he said, "Because he insisted in going off on this very risky endeavor. Into places no one knows well. I thought it might yield some new information about the future, you know. But none of it did any good. He went, and when I questioned his Face a season later, all it would say was that he was under the Ban, the Ban, Bartelmy's Ban. I have no idea what that means. And his quest into the old things is not what I am most interested in." Again that close scrutiny, that casual voice coupled with the tight, attentive body.

Some instinct bade Mavin be still about the other Face

which had also spoken of Bartelmy's Ban. Was it logical that the Wizard would have two such enigmas in his Lake of Faces?

"That surprises me. I was told that the Wizard Chamferton was interested in old things, that he had much information about old things." She pretended astonishment.

"So Himaggery said. Which is why he brought the old women from Betand. Lily-sweet and Rose-love." He paused, then said with elaborate unconcern, "Well, at one time I *was* interested. Very. Oh, yes, at one time I collected such things, delighted in old mysteries. Why, at one time I would probably have been able to tell you everything you wanted to know about the lost road and the tower and the bell. . . ."

Still that impression of testing, of prodding. What was it he wanted her to say? What was it he was worried about her knowing? Mavin chewed, swallowed, thanked the Gamelords that she knew nothing much, but felt herself growing apprehensive nonetheless. She went on, "Do you mention roads, towers, bells by accident? One of the Faces your Harpy questioned spoke of a tower, of bells." She quoted all she could remember of what she had overheard, all in an innocently naive voice, as though she were very little interested.

"Old stories." He dismissed them with a wave of his hand. "The old women Himaggery brought—they were full of old stories." He would have gone on, but the door opened and servants came in to lay the table with steaming food and a tall pitcher of chilled wine. Bunwit and birds, raw or roasted, were all very well, but Mavin had no objection to kitchen food. She pulled her chair close and talked little until the emptiness inside her was well filled.

"Well," she said finally, when the last dish had been emptied—long after Chamferton had stopped eating and taken to merely watching her, seemingly amazed at her appetite; long after the mind tickle had stopped completely, as whoever it was gave up the search—"I must learn what I can from you, Wizard. Himaggery is my friend. I am told by a friend of us both that he came in search of Chamferton because he desired to know about old things and it was thought that you had some such knowledge. Now, you say he went from you on some risky expedition you warned him against. The story of my entire life has been spent thus—in pursuit of kin or friends who have gone off in pursuit of some dream or other. I had not thought to spend this year so, but it seems I am called to do it.''

"Why? For mere friendship?'' Prodding again, trying to elicit information.

Mavin laughed, a quick bark of laughter more the sound of a fustigar than a person. "Are friends so numerous you can say 'mere,' Wizard?'' What would she tell him? Well, it would do no harm to tell him what Pantiquod already knew. "A long time ago, a Gamesman helped my younger brother during the plague at Pfarb Durim. You heard of that? Everyone south of King Frogmott of the Marshes heard of it!'' And especially Pantiquod, who caused it, she thought.

"I heard of it,'' he agreed, too quickly.

She pretended not to notice. "Well, I am fond of my brother. So, even if there were no other reason, in balance to that kindness done by this Gamesman, I will do him a kindness in return. He is Himaggery's friend and wants him found.''

The Wizard's tone was dry and ironic, but still with that underlying tone of prying hostility. "Then all this seeking of yours, which you find so wearying, is for the Seer Windlow.''

"That is all we need consider,'' she said definitely, seeming not to notice his use of a name she had not mentioned. So, Himaggery had talked of his personal life to this Wizard. Of his life? His friends? Perhaps of her? "Anything beyond that would be personal and irrelevant.''

"Very well then,'' he replied. "For the Seer Windlow, I will tell you everything I can.''

As he talked, she grew more certain there was something here unspoken, something hidden, and she little liked the feel of it. However, she did not interrupt him or say anything to draw attention to herself, merely waiting to see what his voice would say which his words did not.

"Himaggery came here, eight years ago. Not in spring, but in the downturn of the year with leaves blowing at his heels and a chilly wind howling in the chimney while we talked. He had a map with him, an interesting one with some features on it I didn't know of though they were near me in these hills. He told me about Windlow, too, and the old books they had searched. Himaggery had been collecting folk tales for six or seven years at that point. He wanted to hear the ones I knew, and I told him he might have full liberty of the library I had collected. Old things are not what I am most interested in now. Now I am interested in the future! It has endless fascination! Himaggery admitted as much, but he didn't share my enthusiasm. Nonetheless, we talked, he told me what he had found in the books, and we dined together and even walked together in the valley for the day or two he spent here. I took a mask from him for the Lake of Faces, which amused him mightily." He fell silent, as though waiting for her to contradict him, but Mavin kept her face innocent and open.

"So! What sent him on? Where did he go from here?"

"Ah. Well, truthfully, he found very little helpful here. I was able to tell him about the road. There is a Road south of Pfarb Durim, with Monuments upon it. Do you know the place? Yes? Well, so did he. And when I told him that the Road goes on, north of Pfarb Durim, hidden under the soil of the ages, north into the Dorbor Range, then swinging west to emerge at the surface in places—when I told him that, he was all afire to see it." He nodded at her, waving his hands to demonstrate the enthusiasm with which Himaggery was supposed to have received this information. "Like a boy. All full of hot juice."

There was something false in this telling, but she would not challenge it. She sought to pique his interest, perhaps to arouse enthusiasm which would override his careful talk. "The Road south of Pfarb Durim that has Monuments on it— I saw them dance, once. The shadowpeople made them do it."

"So Himaggery said! You were there then? I would like to have seen that. . . ."

"My point, Wizard, is that we were not harmed. Some are said to have been driven mad by the Monuments, though I don't know the truth of that, but I have never heard that any were killed. Yet you told Himaggery it was risky? Dangerous?"

"So I believed." He poured half a glass of wine, suddenly less confiding, almost reticent, as though they had approached a subject he had not planned for.

"Come now. You must tell me more than that. You know something more than that. Or believe you do."

"You are persistent," he said in a tone less friendly, lips tight. "Uncomfortably persistent."

Mavin held out her open hands, palms up, as though she juggled weights, put on her most ingenuous face. "Am I to risk my own life, perhaps Himaggery's as well, rather than be discourteous? If it is something which touches you close to the bone, forgive me, Wizard. But I must ask!"

"Very well." He thought it over for a time, hiding his hesitation by moving to the window, opening it to lean out. There he seemed to find inspiration, for he returned with his mouth full of words once more. "There are many stories about the old road, Mavin. Tales, myths—who knows. Well, I had a . . . brother, considerably younger than I. He was adventurous, loved digging into old things like your friend Himaggery. I was away from the demesne when he decided to seek out the mysteries of the old road. I did not even know he had gone until much later, and my own search for him was futile."

"Ah," said Mavin, examining him closely, still keeping her voice light and unchallenging. "So, if the truth were told, Wizard, perhaps you did not warn Himaggery so much as you might? Perhaps, respecting him as you did, you thought he might find your brother for you?"

"Perhaps," he said with easy apology. "Perhaps that is it. I have searched my mind on that subject more times than I care to remember. But I do remember warning him, not once but many times. And I do remember cautioning him, not once but often. And so I put myself to rest, only to doubt again on the morning. I believe I did warn him sufficiently, Shape-shifter. But he chose to go."

She rose in her turn to investigate the open window. It looked out upon the valley, moonlit now, and peaceful. A cool wind moved the budding trees. Scents of spring rose around her, and she sighed as she closed the casement against the cool and turned back into the firelight. "Your Harpy questioned three of the Faces, Wizard. One was an old woman who spoke of a bell. What does it mean, 'The daylight bell hangs in the last tower'?"

He gestured to say how unimportant a question it was. "I told you Himaggery brought two old story-tellers with him from Betand. I took a Face from one of them—her name was Rose-love—shortly before she died. It was her Face you heard in the lake, saying words from a children's story. Old Rose-love told stories to the children of Betand during a very long life, stories of talking foxes and flying fish and of Weetzie and the daylight bell.

"Weetzie?" She laughed, an amused chirrup of sound.

He barked an echoing laugh, watching her closely the while. "Weetzie. And the daylight bell, not an ordinary bell, but something very ancient. Himaggery had heard of it, and of another one. He called it 'the bell of the dark,' the 'cloud bell,' the 'bell of the shadows.' Have you heard of that?" His voice was friendly, yet she felt something sinister in the question, and she mocked herself for feeling so, here in this quiet room with the fire dancing on the hearth. The man had said nothing, done nothing to threaten her. Why this feeling? She forced herself to shake her head, smilingly. No, she had not heard of it.

He went on, "Nor had I. Well, he had found out something about these mysterious bells from old Rose. I question her Face once or twice a year to see how long it will continue to reply. It says only the one thing. First a little verse, then 'The daylight bell hangs in the last tower.' "

"The Blue Star is on the horns of Zanbee."

"It is not," he said. "That time is just past and will not return for many seasons yet." His voice was harsh as he demanded, "Where did you hear that?"

She remained nonchalant. "It was something Himaggery said once. The night the Monuments danced on the Ancient Road south of Pfarb Durim. They danced when the Blue Star was on the horns of Zanbee—the crescent moon. Now we have, 'The bell is in the last tower.' They both sound mysterious, like Wizardly things."

He relaxed. "I suppose they are Wizardly things, in a sense. Certainly your friend Himaggery thought so. My . . . brother, too."

"What was his name?" asked Mavin, suddenly curious about this unnamed brother. "Was he a Wizard?"

"Ah . . . no. No, he was not a Wizard. He was . . . a Time-reacher. Very much a Timereacher." He smiled, something meant to be a kindly smile, at which Mavin shuddered, speaking quickly to hide it.

"His name?"

"Arkhur. He was . . . ah . . . quite young."

"And so, Wizard." She rose, smiling at him, letting the smile turn into a yawn to show how little concerned she was with what she said or what he replied. "You can tell me only that there is a road northwest of this place. That there is a bell somewhere, called variously, which Himaggery talked of. That Himaggery's Face says only what I heard it say. That your brother Arkhur is gone since his youth. That all of this, you think, is connected with ancient things, old things, things beyond memory. You think. You believe."

"And that it is risky, Mavin. Dangerous . . . "

"Everywhere I have gone they have told me that. 'It is risky, Mavin. Dangerous.' I have sought Eesties and battled gray oozers and plotted with stickies and crept through Blourbast's halls in the guise of a snake. All of it was risky, Wizard. I wish you could tell me something more. It is little enough to go on."

"If you had not interrupted me, I would have gone on to say there are others seeking the road you seek." He seemed to wait for her comment or question, to be dissatisfied by her silence. "Also, the other old woman brought here by Himaggery still lives, still chatters, still tells her stories. It is too late to disturb her old bones tonight, but if you will wait until morning, she will tell you one of her stories, no doubt. Perhaps there is something in her story which will enlighten you."

You mean, she thought, that perhaps it will convince me of your friendship, Chamferton, and make me talk more freely. Well, little enough I know, old fox, but I will not tell you more than I need.

She nodded acceptance of the invitation to hear the storyteller, weary to her own bones. The night before had not been restful, and since she had drunk those last few sips of wine she had been weighted down with sleep. She bowed, an ordinary gesture of respect. He patted her on her shoulder, seeming not to feel her flesh flinch away from him, and then tugged the bell near his hand.

Chamferton's servants took her to a room with a bed far softer than her bed of moss had been. There was a tub full of hot water on a towel before the fire. She did not linger in it. The shutters were open at the high window, letting the night air flood the room to chill her wet skin, and she shut them, fumbling with the latch to be sure it would not blow open again. She remembered only fleetingly that Chamferton had spoken of someone else on the trail she followed, thinking that curiosity over this might keep her awake. It did not. She did not even dry herself completely before falling asleep between the sheets, as though drugged.

Chapter 3

Very early in the morning, just before dawn, she woke thinking she had heard some sound—a scratching, prying sound. She sat up abruptly, calling out some question or threat. The shutters were open, a curtain waving between them like a beckoning hand, and she rose, only half awake, to look outside. Around the window were thick vine branches, one of which was pulled away from the wall, as though something heavy had tried to perch upon it. She saw it without seeing it, for in the yard at the base of the stairs a group of horsemen was preparing to depart. Even with her eyes Shifted, she could not make out their faces in the dim light, but there was something familiar about one of them—something in the stance. Chamferton she could identify by his tall hat, and he stood intimately close to the familiar figure, their two heads together in conspiratorial talk. Mavin widened her ears, heard only scattered phrases. " . . . While she is here . . . easy enough to get rid of . . . "

Then the horses walked away, not hurrying their pace until they had gone well down the valley, and Mavin knew it was for quiet's sake, so that she would not hear. "Shifter ears, Wizard," she yawned. "Never try to fool Shifter's ears."

43

After watching the men ride out of sight, she closed the shutters firmly once more, then returned to bed to sleep until the sun was well up.

In the late morning she found Chamferton on a pleasant terrace behind the plinth on which the castle stood. There she ate melons grown under glass, the Wizard said, so they ripened even in the cold season. He was all smiling solicitude this morning, and Mavin might have accepted it from one who did not employ Harpies as servants. They were creatures of such malice, she could not believe good of one who kept them, though she asked him whether the injured Harpy lived, trying to sound as though she cared.

"Foulitter is recovering," he told her. "She bears you much malice. Or perhaps me, for not punishing you. I told her her former plots against me earned her whatever damage you had done to her, and to hush and do my bidding." He smiled at Mavin, showing his teeth, which were stained and crooked. It was not a nice smile, and she did not find it reassuring.

"I would not like to have her behind me when I go," said Mavin, cursing herself silently for having said so the moment the words left her mouth.

"I will see she does not leave the aerie for some time," he promised with that same smile. "She is fully under my control. I am less worried about her than about some others who seek the same road you do."

Mavin put down her spoon with a ringing sound which hung upon the air. "You mentioned that last night. I was so weary, I could not even think to ask who it would be."

"Did you ever meet King Prionde's eldest heir? Valdon Duymit, son of the King Prionde?" His voice was deceptively casual, as it had been the night before.

Valdon! Of course. That had been the familiar stance she had recognized. So. Valdon had been the Wizard's guest until the predawn hours—and he had left surreptitiously. She deducted another portion from Chamferton's reputation for truth. Do not say too much, Mavin, she instructed herself. But do not lie, for he may know part of the truth already. "I have," she admitted. "I was there when he and Himaggery came almost to Game duel between them. They did not like one another."

"So much I guessed," he said. "Nonetheless, he came here, so he said, in search of Himaggery."

"Did he say why?" She spooned up melon, trying not to seem interested in the answer to this question.

"Oh, he gave me some reason or other. He lied. However, I encourage my servants to gossip. Sometimes it is the only way to get at the truth. My servants told me he fancied himself wronged for some reason connected with the school set up by Prionde. Do you know anything about that?"

"I know of the school, yes." She spoke of it as anyone might who knew nothing beyond its location and that Prionde had sponsored it, thinking meantime that it was undoubtedly the Harpy whom he counted upon to gossip among the guests. In her own shape, she was probably not uncomely.

"So I had some knowledge of the school," she concluded, "though I am told it is not a large one. That is all I know."

"You are succinct. Would that more of my informants were so terse. Well, I gathered that Valdon has some unfinished anger which moves him. He desires Himaggery's embarrassment, perhaps even his destruction. I knew that. I could read it in his voice; I did not need a Face from him to learn it." An expression of annoyance crossed the Wizard's face, was wiped away in an instant as though he became aware of it and did not want the world to see it.

"How long ago was Valdon here?"

"Oh, a year or two. No. Little more than a year. I tell you so you may be warned." He turned toward the stairs while Mavin made note he had told her yet another lie.

"Ah. Look over there to the steps. See the old woman, the very old woman being carried up in the chair? She is two hundred years old, that woman. So she says, and so I do believe. Old as rocks, as the country people say. That is Lily-sweet, sister to Rose-love, whose Face you saw in my lake. I have had her carried up here in the sun, which she much enjoys, and promised her all the melon she can eat if she will tell you a story. She and her sister told stories in Betand for all their long lives, stories learned from their great grandmas, who also, if the stories about them be true, lived to be very old. If she were still young and strong, she could talk about Weetzie for several days, for Weetzie had more adventures than a thousand years would have given him time for. Somewhere in all that mass of story-telling is a little verse which says something about there being a road, and on the road a tower, and in the tower a bell, which cannot ring alone. That verse much intrigued your friend Himaggery. You may choose to ask for the story of Weetzie and the daylight bell. She will say she is too old to remember, too tired, that it is only a children's story, a country tale. You must persist." He was playing with her now, Mavin knew. All this was so much flummery, to keep her occupied.

"This is the story you mentioned last night."

"Yes. If you seek Himaggery, you may find something in it. He pretended to do so. If you are to get her to tell you anything you must say her name in full, caressingly, and do not laugh." Chamferton went back to his melon, waving her away.

She rose almost unwillingly, strongly tempted to challenge his lies and his foisting nonsense upon her in the guise of information, and yet unwilling to pass by anything in which Himaggery had been interested. That much, at least, might be true and she, Mavin, might find help in it that Chamferton did not intend. So she strolled across the high terrace to the chair where the old woman sat wrapped in knitted shawls against the slight chill of the morning. She was so old her face and arms were wrinkled like the shell of a nut, like the fine wavelets of a sea barely brushed by wind. Thin flesh hung from her arms and neck. Wisps of white hair fringed the edge of her cap. Her eyes were bird-bright though she pretended not to see Mavin's approach. "Well then," thought Mavin, "we will lure her as the birder does the shy fowl of the air".

"Lily-sweet," she begged, "the High Wizard Chamferton says that you know a tale known to none other in all the lands. The tale of Weetzie and the daylight bell."

The old woman stroked her throat, made a pitiful shrug and shook her head wistfully. "Ah, girl, but one's throat is too dry and old for telling tales."

Mavin rose without a word and went to Chamferton's table. "I need to borrow a teacup," she told him, returning with it to the old woman.

"Wet your gullet, Lily-sweet. This is the High Wizard's own

tea, and while it is not good enough for softening the throat of a true story-teller, still, it is the best we have."

"You are a well spoken child, for all your outlandish appearance. In my day the women wore full trews and vests to show their bosoms. None of this tight man-breeching and loose shirts." Lily-sweet tugged at Mavin's shirt, and inside that tug, Mavin twitched. The shirt was herself.

"So my own grandmama has said, Lily-sweet. And much we regret that those days are past." She sighed. "If we dressed now as true women did in the days of your youth, chance is I would have a . . . companion of my own."

"You'd have a husband, child, and thankful for it. Ah, and well, and sorry the day. What was it you wanted to know of again?"

"The story of Weetzie and the daylight bell?"

"Ah. A children's story, was it? I'm not sure I remember that one."

"Oh, it would be a tragedy if you did not, Lily-sweet, for none but you can be found to tell it rightly. Oh, there are those in Betand who pretend to know the story, but the mockery they make of it is quite . . . "

"None know that story save me!" The voice was suddenly more definite, and the old hands quivered upon the arms of the chair. "Since sister Rose died, none but me."

"I know," Mavin soothed. "So says the Wizard Chamferton. He says the women in Betand are liars and scrape-easies, that you are the only one who has the truth of it."

"And so I do," said the old woman. "And so shall you be the judge of it." She took a deep breath.

"One time," she quavered, gesturing with a claw to indicate a time long past, "one time a time ago, was a young star named Weetzie, and he went out and about, up and down, wet and dry, come day come night till he got to the sea. And there was a d'bor wife, grodgeling about in the surf, slither on slither.

"And Weetzie spoke polite to her, saying 'Good morn to you, d'bor wife. And why do you slither here near the shore when the deep waves are your home?'

"And the d'bor wife, she struck at him once, twice, three times with her boaty flappers, flap, flap, flap on the sand, but

Weetzie jumped this way and that way, and all that flapping was for nothing. So, seeing she could not get Weetzie that way, the d'bor wife began to sing in her lure voice, 'Oh, I grodgel here in the surf to find the daylight bell where the shadows hid it.'

"And Weetzie was greatly taken with this idea, so he came close to the d'bor wife and began to help her grodgel. And whup, the d'bor wife wrapped Weetzie up in her short reachers and laughed like a whoop-owl, 'Oh, little star, but I have you now, I have you now.'

"And Weetzie was sorry to have been so silly, for Weetzie's forepeople had often said that trusting a d'bor was like betting on the wind. So Weetzie thought quick, quick, and said, 'But why did you stop me, d'bor wife? Quick, grodgel down, grodgel down, for just as you caught me, I saw the very edge of the daylight bell.'

"And the d'bor wife was so excited, she dropped Weetzie in the instant and began to grodgel again, with the water flying. And Weetzie took his bone and twanged it, so the d'bor wife was all wound up in her tentacles and tied in a lump. Then he sat down and sang this song:

'Daylight bell in water can't be;
Tricksy lie brings tricksy tie.
Give a boon or else you die.'

"And the d'bor wife cried loudly, until all the seabirds shrieked to hear it, and begged the little star to be let go. So Weetzie said, 'Give me the boon, d'bor wife, and I'll untie you.'

"So they talked and talked while the sun got high, and this was the boon: that Weetzie could go in the water and breathe there as did the d'bor. So he twanged his bone to turn the d'bor wife loose and went on his way, up and down, over and under, back and forth in the wide world until he came to a forest full of tall trees.

"And there in the top of the tallest tree was a flitchhawk in a nest, grimbling and grambling at the clouds as they flew past. And Weetzie cried out, 'Ho there, flitchhawk, why are you grimbling and grambling at the clouds?' And the flitchhawk said, 'Because I'm looking for the daylight bell which is hung up here in the mist where the shadows hid it.'

" 'I'll help you, then,' cried Weetzie, and he climbed the tall tree 'til he came high up, and he stood in the nest and reached out for the clouds to grimble and gramble them in pieces. But the flitchhawk screamed and grabbed Weetzie in his huge claws and then laughed and cawed as though to raise the dark, 'Little star, I've got you now.'

" 'Why did you grab me, old flitchhawk,' cried Weetzie, 'just as I was grambling the clouds? I caught a glimpse of the daylight bell just there where I was grambling when you took hold of me!' And when he heard that, the flitchhawk dropped Weetzie and went back to grimbling and grambling the clouds, looking for the daylight bell and crying, 'Where is it? Where did you see it?' But Weetzie took his bone and twanged it and sang this song:

'Daylight bell in water can't be
Daylight bell in treetop shan't be
Tricksy lie brings tricksy tie.
Give a boon or else you die.'

"And flitchhawk was tied wing and claw so he couldn't move, and he begged to be let loose, but Weetzie would not until the flitchhawk gave him a boon. And the boon was that Weetzie could fly in the wide sky as the flitchhawk had always done. So then Weetzie twanged his bone and turned the flitchhawk loose.

"Up and down he went, in and out, under and over, until time wore on, and Weetzie came to a broad plain where there was a gobble-mole druggling tunnels, coming up with a snoutful of dirt and heaving it into little hillocks. So, Weetzie said, 'What's all the tunneling for old gobble? More tunnel there than a mole needs in a million.'

"And the gobble-mole says, 'Druggling to find the daylight bell, little star. I know it's right down here somewhere in the deep earth where the shadows hid it.'

"So Weetzie says, 'Well, then, I'll help you druggle for it,' and he started in to druggle with the mole. But the mole pushed Weetzie in a hole and shut it up so Weetzie couldn't get out.

"And Weetzie cried, 'What did you do that for, old mole? I caught sight of the edge of the daylight bell, just then, before you covered it up with your druggling.'

"Old mole said, 'Where? Where did you see it?' and he un-covered the hole where Weetzie was so Weetzie could twang his bone and sing this song:

'Daylight bell in water can't be
Daylight bell in treetop shan't be
Daylight bell in earthways wan't be
Tricksy lie brings tricksy tie.
Give a boon or else you die.

"And the gobble-mole was all tied up, foot and snout, so he couldn't move. So the gobble-mole decided upon a boon, and the boon was that Weetzie should be able to walk in earthways as the mole had always done. Then Weetzie twanged his bone and let the mole loose.

" 'Well now,' said Weetzie. 'All this talk of the daylight bell has made me curious, so I'll take my three boons and go look-ing for it.' And all the creatures within ear-listen laughed and laughed, for none had ever found the daylight bell where the shadows had hidden it, though the beasts had had boons of their own for ever since. But Weetzie danced on the tip of himself, up and down, in and out, over and under, as he went seeking."

The old woman sighed. Mavin put the teacup to her lips, and she sipped the pale brew, sighing again. "That's the story of Weetzie and the daylight bell, girl."

"Is there more to the story, Lily-sweet?"

"Oh, there's enough for three days' telling, girl, for it may be he found the bell at the end of it, but I'm weary of it now. Let be. He that calls himself Wizard there may tell it to you if you've a mind to hear it. I told it to him, and to that other Wizard—real, he was, sure as my teeth are gone—and to people in Betand, and to children many a time when they were no more than mole-high themselves." And she leaned back in the chair, shutting her eyes. So the old woman did not much care for Chamferton, either. "He that calls himself Wiz-ard . . ."

Back at the table where Chamferton sat smiling at her as a fox might smile at a bird, she continued to play the innocent. "I wonder what all that was about?"

"I think it's about Eesties, Shifter-woman, though I'm not certain of that. Eesties, Eestnies, the Old-folk, the Rolling

Stars. Whatever you choose to call them . . . ''

"They say 'Eesty' among themselves," said Mavin, without thinking. Then her throat closed like a vice and she coughed, choking, gesturing frantically for air.

"You mean you've spoken to them, seen them? Gamelords, girl, tell me of it!" His face blazed with an acquisitive glow, and his hand clutched her arm. *Now*, she thought through her suffocating spasm, *now* I see the true Chamferton.

She shook her head, trying to breathe as her face turned blue. Then the spasm passed, and he nodded with comprehension, handing her a cup. "Don't try to talk then. I understand. What you've seen, what you've heard, they don't want talked about. Well. Pity." He took paper from a nearby table and wrote on it, "Have you ever tried to write it out?" He turned the paper for her to read.

She shook her head, drawing deep breaths as her throat opened reluctantly.

He put the pen and paper near her hand. She wrote a trial sentence. "I have talked with an Eesty at Ganver's Grave. . . ." Nothing happened. She turned the paper to face him, and he nodded eagerly.

"Well, Shifter-girl, there is a bit of additional information which I will trade you for an account of your . . . experience." He nodded toward her hand, resting upon the paper as he turned the page toward her again. He had written, "If you will write me an account of your experience, I will tell something else about Himaggery—also, I will pay you well for the account."

Mavin shook her head in pretended indecision. "You know, Wizard, from time to time I have been asked to Game for this King or that Sorcerer. All have offered to pay me well, but none has yet told me what I am to do with the pay. What do Shifters need, after all? I cannot eat more than one meal at once, nor sleep in more than one bed at a time. I have little need to array myself in silks or gems. What payment would mean something to me?"

"Perhaps hospitality," he suggested. "A place to rest, or eat cooked food, or merely to stare at the hills."

"No. It is not tempting," she said, having already decided what she would give him which might both allay his suspicions of her and make him careless. "But I will do it because you have something to tell me about Himaggery, and for no other reason."

He nodded, then remarked in passing, almost as though it did not matter. "And—when you go to seek Himaggery, will you seek Arkhur as well? At least, do not close your eyes to him if you see him on the road? And if you see any sign of him, will you send word to me? Again, though it may take time to agree upon a coin, I will pay you well."

She smiled. Let him take that for assent if he would. She would do no more than write what she had seen of the Eesties and of the dancing Monuments and the shadowpeople upon the hills. She made it brief, leaving most of what had happened out, unwilling to put anything in his hands he might use for ill—as he would. She did mention that the magical talisman, Ganver's Bone, had been taken back by the Eesty who gave it, believing that it would go ill for the shadowpeople if Chamferton thought they still had it, though why she was so certain of that, she could not have said. When she had finished, it was a very brief account, though Chamferton nodded his head over it, almost licking his lips, when she had finished.

"This goes in my library, Mavin." Then, after a pause, as though to assure her of his good intent. "And should you not return in a fairly short time, I'll see that a copy of it goes to Windlow."

She nodded, in a sober mood. If she did not return in a fairly short time, she doubted Windlow could do much about it. Also, she thought Chamferton would not bother to do anything, no matter what he had promised, unless for some reason of his own. "I'm off north, now, Wizard, so tell me now what thing it is you know."

For a moment she thought he would deny the bargain, but he thought better of it. "It is only this one fact, Shifter. There are runners upon the road to the north. Strange runners. They come in silence, fleeing along the Ancient Road, without speaking. It was those runners Himaggery followed, and if you see them, they may lead you to the place he went."

So. She wondered what else he might have told her if he had wished to. How much he had left untold. How many other things he had lied about. Why say Valdon had not been there for a year when he had left only this morning? Why all that careful questioning, that covert watching? What had he hoped to learn?

Well, she would not find out by moping over it. Of the two of them, Mavin had probably learned the more. She went down and out of the place, the door shutting behind her with an echoing slam of finality. She started to turn toward the north, then whirled at a sound behind her.

It was Pantiquod, in Harpy shape, her head moving rest-lessly on its flexible serpent's neck, and her pale breasts heav-ing with anger. Yellow-eyed Pantiquod. Mavin set herself to fight, ready to Shift in the instant.

"Oh, no, fool Shifter," the Harpy hissed. "I will not attack you here under Chamferton's walls, where he may yet come out and stop me. Nor in the forest's shadow, where you and I might be well matched. No, Shifter-girl. I will come for you with my sisters. When I will. And there will be no more shadowpeople singing to help you, or tame Wizards to do your bidding, nor will Shiftiness aid you against the numbers I will bring."

There was hot, horrid juice in Mavin's throat, but she managed somehow to keep her voice calm. "Why, Panti-quod? What have I done to you? Your daughter is recovering, and it was she who attacked me, not I her."

The Harpy's head wove upon its storklike neck, the square yellowed teeth bared in a hating grimace. "It was you killed Blourbast, though Huld put the knife in his throat. It was you robbed us of Pfarb Durim. It was you and your forest scum friends who sang away the plague, Shifter-girl. Now it is you who has wounded my daughter, Foulitter. Did you think the Harpies would not avenge themselves?"

"You have not done much for twenty years, loathsome chicken," Mavin said. "But threats are easy and promises cheap. Do what you will." Her knees were not as strong as her voice as she turned her back upon the bird, opening a tiny eye in the back of her head to be sure she was not attacked from the rear. Pantiquod merely stood, however, staring after her, her yellow eyes burning as though a fire were lit behind them.

Mavin shivered, not letting it show. When she was a wee child, she had been afraid of snakes. Her worst dreams had been of touching snakes. The Harpy moved her with a similar revulsion. She did not want to be touched by that creature. She could not think of fighting it because she would have to touch it. Still, so long as she could Shift, she could not utterly fear the Harpy—even if there were more than one. So long as she could Shift, it would not pay the sag-breasted bird to attack her.

When she had come out of sight of the tower, she entered the trees. There she crouched upon the ground, looking back the way she had come. Two sets of wings circled high above the tower, moving upward upon warm drafts of air. When they had achieved considerable height, they turned toward her and the wings beat slowly as the two figures closed the distance between them. Though she had not shown fear before Pantiquod, now Mavin watched the wings come nearer with a feeling of fatalistic fascination which paralyzed her, that nightmare horror of childhood, that ancient terror children feel when they awake in the dark, sure that something lurks nearby, so immobilized by that knowledge that they cannot move to escape. Only when the Harpies had come almost within hailing distance did she stir herself, melting back into the shadows and changing her hide into a mottled invisibility of green and brown. There had been something hypnotic in the Harpy's stare, something like . . .

"I would advise you, Mavin," her internal voice said calmly, "that you not look into a Harpy's eyes again. It would be sensible to kill them now, but if you find them too repulsive even for killing, then you should get moving. If you don't want to fight the creatures, avoidance would be easier if they didn't find you."

This broke the spell and she ran, under the boughs, quickly away to the north, deep in small canyons and under the edges of curling cliffs, until she had left the Harpies behind her, or lost them, or they had gone on ahead. In any case, the feeling of paralysis had passed—at least for the time. Her voice had been right. She should have killed them then. "I must be getting old, and weak, and weary," she cursed herself. "Perhaps I should settle on a farm, somewhere, and grow thrilps." This was not convincing, even under the circumstances, and she gave it up. Enough that she had not wanted to touch the beasts. Leave it at that.

She had come some little distance north when she saw the first travelers, paralleling her course to the west. They were higher on the sides of the hills, running with their heads faced forward—though there was something odd about those heads she could not precisely identify, even with sharpened vision, as the forest light dappled and shadowed. They were naked, men and women both, with long, shaggy hair unbound flapping at their backs. At first she saw only four or five of them, but as she went on others could be seen in small groups on the hillsides, emerging into sunlight before disappearing momentarily into shade once more.

There was a sheer wall ahead, one which stretched across her own path and that of those on the hill, a fault line where the land on which she walked had fallen below that to the north, leaving a scarp between, that scarp cut by tumbling streams which had left ladders of stone in their wake. The westernmost such path was also the nearest, and as she went on she saw the others gradually shift direction toward the rock stair, toward her own path, toward intersection. Prudence dictated she not intrude upon a multitude though the multitude seemed utterly unaware of her, so she dawdled a bit, trotting rather than striding, letting the others draw ahead.

When she came at last to the stream bed which led upward to the heights, they were assembled there, squatting on the ground in fives and sevens, small intent circles faced inward. She crept into the trees above them from which she could watch and listen without being observed. Their heads were bent. The chant started so softly she thought she imagined it, then louder, repeated, repeated.

"Upon the road, the old road,
A tower made of stone.
In the tower is a bell
Which cannot ring alone.

One. Two. Three. Four. Five . . . " The voices went on, breathy, counting, seemingly endlessly. At last they faded into silence on number one thousand thirteen, as though exhausted. After a time they began again.

"Shadow bell, it rang the night,
Daylight bell the dawn,
In the tower hung the bells,
Now the tower's gone.
One thousand thirteen, one thousand twelve, one thousand
eleven . . . " and so on until they came to one again.

Some of the heads came up. She saw then what had been so
odd. They were blindfolded, their heads covered as far as their
nostrils with black masks, like flitchhawks upon the wrist,
hooded. They were silent, faced inward, hearing nothing.
Mavin rustled a branch. They did not respond. Then, all at
once, without any signal which she could see, they stood up
and began to run once more, up the stone ladder toward the
heights.

Intrigued, she Shifted into something spidery and went up
the wall in one concerted rush to confront them at the top of
the scarp. They went past her as though she did not exist, not
hearing her challenging cry. She fell in behind them, not
needing to keep up, for their tracks were as plain as a stream
bed before her. There were hundreds of them, sometimes running separately, sometimes together. She set her feet upon
their trail and thought furiously about the matter.

Somehow, without sight, they knew where they were going.
But sometimes they ran together, sometimes not. Therefore,
her curious mind troubled at the thought, therefore? Sometimes the way was single, sometimes separate? Like strands of
rope, raveled in places, twisted tight in others? But where were
the signs of it? She put her nose up and sharpened her eyes.
Whatever it was that guided them, it couldn't be smelled.

Now they were running all together, in one long clump,
straggling a bit, yet with the edges of the group smooth, feet
falling cleanly into the tracks of those before. Something
along the edges, then. She paused beside the track, peering,
scratching with her paws.

Tchah. Nothing she could see. Nothing she could feel. She
stopped, puzzled, scratching her hide where the dirt of the
road itched it. Perhaps from above.

She Shifted, lifted, beat strong wings down to raise her into
the soft air, circling high, above the trees, sharpening sight so
that she could see a tick upon a bunwit's back. Circle higher,

higher, peering down at the runners, separated again now. She could see their trail cleanly upon the earth, a troubling of the grass, a line of broken twigs. Leaves crushed. Dark then light. And more!

Along their way a scattering of stones. No. Not scattered, tumbled. Heaved up. Some washed aside in spring rains, but still maintaining their relationship to one another. Lines of stones. A slightly different shade of gray than the natural stones of the hills. Lighter. Finer grained. Like the stones of the Ancient Road south of Pfarb Durim. She dropped like a plummet, down onto those stones, then Shifted once more.

Yes. Now she could see the difference. But how did the runners know? She laid her palm upon the stone, shut her eyes, concentrated. It was there, a kind of tingling, a small, itchy feeling as of lightning in the air. Experimentally, she Shifted a human foot and laid it upon the stone. Yes. She could feel it. So then. She did not need to follow the runners, she knew where they would go. They would follow this road, this road, broken or solid.

Satisfied, she trotted in the tracks of those who ran, wanting to see what they would do when night came.

Had Himaggery come this way in pursuit of the runners? Or had he followed the map, which would likely have brought him to the same place? And where was that place? A tower, she thought. There is always something magical about a tower, a stone tower. Magicians and Wizards live in towers. Kings are held captive in towers. Signals come from towers, and dragons assault towers. So it is fitting that on this old road there should be a tower. But now the tower's gone. So sang the runners. Then what were they looking for?

"Shadow bell, it rang the night, daylight bell the dawn, in the tower hung the bells, but now the tower's gone," she hummed to herself between fustigar teeth. Not really gone, she thought. Gone, perhaps, but not really gone. Just as Himaggery was gone, but not really gone. Somewhere. Somewhere. Somewhere.

It became a chant, a kind of prayer which accompanied each footfall. Somewhere. Somewhere.

Chapter 4

The way of the Ancient Road lay across hills and valleys, sometimes with the slope, sometimes against it, as though the Road had been there first and the valleys had come later to encroach upon it. Sometimes trotting, sometimes scrambling, Mavin followed the way, the tracks of the runners going on before her, the sun crossing above her to sink into the west so that long bars of shadow stood parallel to her path, making a visible road along which she and the runners moved in a silence broken only by far, plaintive birdsong. Beside the road bloomed brilliant patches of yellow startle flower—no seedpods yet to startle the traveler with noonday explosions. Beneath them lay the leafy lacework of Healer's balm, a promise that great purple bells would swing above the moss toward the end of the season. Clouds had sailed in from the west all day, full of the threat of rain, but none had fallen. Instead the gray billows had gone on eastward to pile themselves into a featureless veil covering the Dorbor Range. The east was all storm and rumbling thunder while the west glowed softly in sunset. The shadow road was as clear before her as an actual road would have been.

It was a moment before she realized that she ran upon the surface of an actual roadway. In this place the tingling stones had never been covered, or perhaps they had come up out of time to lie upon the earth once more. Among the trees she could catch glimpses on either side of huge, square stones which might once have supported monuments like those which arched the road outside Pfarb Durim. The light glared straight into her eyes from the horizon, blinding her, and she almost strode across the naked runners before she saw them. They lay upon the roadway, prostrate in their hundreds. She stood for a moment, troubled at the sight of so many figures lying as though dead upon the road, barely breathing.

The light faded into dusky gray-purple. The runners heaved themselves onto all fours and crawled into the surrounding forest, scavenging among the litter on the forest floor for the moist carpets of fungus which lay in every sunny glade. Seeing them moving about, Mavin felt less pity for them and set to follow their example, making a pouch in her hide to gather this crop as well. The mushrooms were both delicious and nourishing, known among gourmands as "earth's ears" both for their shape and raw texture, crisp and cartilaginous. Both the flavor and texture improved when they were cooked, which Mavin intended to do. The sight of the runners groveling offended her, and only after she had found a place to suit her remote from them did she build a fire at last, laying the wood against a cracked stony shelf beside a small pool. Her firestarter was the only tool she carried, the only tool she needed to carry—though she had heard it said in Danderbat Keep that one Flourlanger Obquisk had learned to Shift flint and steel in some long forgotten time. Mavin had never believed it a practical solution. Since one would have to Shift flint and steel into one's body to begin with, why not simply carry them and have done.

She sat warming herself, lengthening her fur to hold body heat from the evening cool, turning the thin sticks on which the fungus was strung, watching it crisp and brown. A strange sound pervaded the quiet, a soft whirring, as though some giant top hummed to itself nearby. She crouched, trying to decide whether it conveyed some threat, whether the fire should be put out or she herself put remote from it. She compromised by leaping to the top of the shelf and collapsing there into a pancake of flesh, invisible upon the stony height.

Something came into the clearing, a whirlwind, a spinning cloud, a silvery teardrop gyring upon its tip. It glinted in the light of the fire, twirling, slowing, the long silver fringes of its dress falling out of their spiral swirl into a column, the outstretched arms coming to rest, one hand clasped lightly in another. It wore a round silver hat from which another fringe settled, completely hiding the face—if there was a face.

Upon the stone, Mavin stirred in astonishment and awe. She had never seen a Dervish before, for they were rare and solitary people, devoted, it was said, to strange rites in the worship of ancient gods. Still, she could not fail to recognize what stood there, for the dress and habits of Dervishes figured often in children's tales and fireside stories. Wonderful, remote, and marvelous they were said to be, but she had never heard they were malign. She dropped from the side of the stone and came around it to the fire once more, reaching to turn the splints on which the mushrooms roasted. Let it speak if it would.

"I smelled your fire," it said. Mavin could not tell if it was man or woman, for the voice was scarcely more than a whisper. "The runners build no fire, so I knew someone followed them. I came to warn."

Mavin chose to disregard the warning. "Will you sit down?" Mavin gestured at a likely rock beside the flames. "I would be glad to share my supper."

"Thank you, no. I seldom sit. I seldom eat. Like those poor runners on the road, I go on and on, without thinking about it very much." There was a breathy sound beneath these words which, after a time, Mavin interpreted as laughter.

"My name is Mavin," she offered. "Mavin Manyshaped."

"A Shifter," the other breathed. "I could tell from your fur. A pretty beast, you, Mavin Manyshaped. An unusual one as well. Most beasts do not cook their earth's ears."

"They taste better cooked," said Mavin, testing one with her fingers to see if it was done. "Also, when they are cooked, they do not make that noise between one's teeth that makes one believe one is eating something still alive and resisting."

"Ah," laughed the windy voice, "a pretty, sensitive beast. Are you following the runners?"

"I am." She saw no need for dissimulation. "I am seeking someone—someone who followed these runners eight years ago. Someone who has not been seen since, but who the Rancelmen and Pursuivants say still lives. Have you seen him?"

The figure before her shrugged. "Perhaps, Mavin Manyshaped. I have seen many since first I watched the runners go past. That time, the first time, they sang nine hundred years and twenty. This time they sing one thousand and thirteen. In that time, I have seen many, Mavin Manyshaped."

Mavin set the splint to one side to cool a little. "These runners—they run each year?"

"Each year, beginning when the Blue Star approaches the horns of Zanbee, from the south city upon the Ancient Road, north, west, then south and east until they come to the south city once more. Many die upon the way, of course. Every year, many die."

"The road makes a circle?"

"A circuit. Yes."

"And where is the south city?"

"It is only ruins now. A place in the hills, at the headwaters of the River Banner, north of Mip and Pouws. Do you know that land?"

"I never heard of any ruined city there."

"No. They hide it well, these devotees. Still, when the Blue Star rises, they assemble in that place for the run. Those who die upon the circuit are assured of bliss, so they say. Even those who live to return to the lands of the south have earned great merit."

"But . . . " Mavin took a mouthful of mushroom and sucked in the juice which spurted on her lips. "What is it all for?"

There was that hint of breathy laughter once more. "What is it for? What is anything for, Mavin Manyshaped. There is something in their eschatology which speaks of rebuilding the tower. You will say, 'What tower?' and I will say, 'What tower, indeed?' " The Dervish paused, seeming to invite response or comment.

Mavin felt the question, chose not to indicate interest. "The tower that is gone, I suppose," she said flatly. "Except that it isn't gone. I think."

"What makes you think that?"

Now there was no mistaking the oddly expectant tone in that whispery voice. As though they had been talking in riddles. As though the Dervish were seeking some particular answer. Mavin decided to let the matter go no further. If Dervishes were not malign, still they were not understood. Least said, best handled. For now.

She nodded over her meal. "Oh, just that it seems likely there must be some tower around someplace or other. Sufficient to keep the legends spinning. Don't you think?"

Something wilted in the Dervish's stance. Still, it persisted. "Have you come this way before, Mavin Manyshaped? Upon this road? Or any other?"

Surprised by the question, Mavin answered it honestly. "I have not come this way before, Dervish." She finished chewing, swallowing. "Now. Dervish without a name, can you help me find the one I seek?"

"Perhaps," said the Dervish with a disappointed breath. "Perhaps." It began to spin, at first slowly, arms rising until they were straight out from the shoulders, fringes rising, whirling, the figure moving faster and faster. When the fringe rose from the face, Mavin caught a look at it, skeletally thin, huge-eyed, lips curved in an eternal, unchanging expression of calm, and yet—Mavin thought she saw something of disappointment in the face, too, though it blurred into motion too quickly for her to be sure. The Dervish hummed, spun, began to move away through the trees. Mavin let it go.

"If you will, perhaps," she whispered to herself, "then do, perhaps. Though why you should have expected me to say anything else, I do not know. So, if you will help me find him, do. If not . . . well, I will find him by myself." She lay back upon the mosses, replete, weary, now suddenly full of new thoughts. If the Ancient Road merely bent upon itself and returned to the south, then was Himaggery likely upon it or aside from it? Would he—could he have joined the runners? She would not have thought to look for him there.

Groaning, she rose to her feet and made a torch to light her way. Back upon the road the runners lay sprawled, unconscious, driven into exhausted sleep. She moved among them, making an orderly pattern in her mind to assure that she examined them all. Men, women, even some who were little more than children. Lean as old leather straps, bruised and scratched from the road, with soles on their feet like cured d'bor skin, hard as wood. She turned over lax bodies, pulled hoods aside to peer into faces, and replaced them. There were hundreds of them, and the task took hours. Dawn paled the eastern sky before she was finished. The clouds of the night before had gone; now there was only clear sky to the eastern horizon, flushed with sickly rose. Mavin threw down the torch with a growl of disgust and wandered back to her fire to curl close around the coals and sleep, not caring that the runners woke, chanted, and ran on into the west. She could find them if she wanted to. She was no longer sure she wanted to.

Late evening she wakened, stretched, scratched, built up her fire once more, gathered a new supply of earth's ears thinking furiously the while. Himaggery had followed the runners. He had come, as she had, to this place on the road. Likely he, as she, had encountered the Dervish. The Dervish who had "come to warn." The Dervish who had said that the runners would return to the south would likely have said as much to Himaggery. Who had not, at that time, joined the runners. At least he was not among them now. So he had turned aside, say.

"As good a supposition as any other," she encouraged herself. Himaggery had turned aside, then, after meeting the Dervish. Why?

"Because," she answered herself, "he, too, would have said something about the tower. Being Himaggery, he would not have done as I did, merely put the subject aside. No, he would have said something curious, something more Wizardly than mere chitchat. And if he did, then the Dervish would have replied with something sensible, also, and off Himaggery would have gone. So. Perhaps. At least it is worthy of examining further." She covered the fire with earth and Shifted into fustigar shape. The Dervish would not be difficult to track.

The trail was like a swept path, leaves and litter blown to either side by the Dervish's spinning, a little drift on either side marking the way. The path led away north of the road, down quiet moon-silvered glens and through shadowed copses, up long, dark inclines where the black firs sighed in the little wind, quietly moving as in the depths of a silent sea. Though

e way rose and fell, she was neither climbing nor descending
verall. Streams fell from higher tablelands into the valleys,
an there as quick streams away into the lowlands beyond. She
ove deeper and deeper into the hills.

She could not recall ever having come that way before, and
et there was something familiar about a distant crest, the way
a which a line of mountain cut another beside a great pin-
acle. There was something recognizable in the way a bulky
liff edged up into the moonlight, catching the rays upon one
mooth face so that it glowed like a mirror in the night. She
topped, tried to think where she had seen it before. It must
ave been some other similar place, though it teased at her,
licking at the edges of memory.

From this place the trail led upward, over a ridge. On either
ide were great trees, those called the midnight tree because of
ts black leaves and silver bark. The trees were rare, had
lways been rare, and were rarer now because of men's in-
atiable use of the black and silver wood, beautiful as a
veaving of silk. Mavin shook her head, troubled. She had
een . . . seen such trees before. Not—not from this angle, but
he bulk of them seemed somehow familiar, painful, as
hough connected with something she did not want to remem-
er. Still, the trail led between the trees and down.

Down. There was velvet moss beneath her feet. She could
eel it, smell it. The moss was starred with tiny white blossoms
vhich breathed sweetness into the night. Other blossoms hung
n long, graceful panicles from the trees, and a spice vine
wined up a stump beside the way. Here the Dervish had
lowed, stopped spinning. He—she, it had walked here
juietly, scarcely leaving a trail. Across the valley was a low
tone wall, and behind that wall a small building. Mavin could
ot see it, but she knew it was there. Discomfited, she whined,
he fustigar shape taking over for a moment to circle on the
ragrant moss, yelping its discomfort. Across the valley a
ombi roared, softly, almost gently, like a drum roll.

The fustigar fell silent, Shifted up into Mavin herself, wide-
yed and bat-eared upon the night, no less uncomfortable but
nore reasoning in her own shape. "Now, now," she soothed
erself. "Come now. It may be enchantment, or some malign
nfluence or some Game you know nothing of, Mavin. Hold

tight. Go down slowly, slowly, into this valley." Which sh
did, step by step, pausing after each to listen and sniff the air

A pool opened at her side, ran lilting into another. The pa
crossed still another on a bridge of stone which curved upwa
like a lover's kiss. Down through the blossoming trees sh
could see the valley floor, laced with streamlets and pools, li
a silver filigree in the light. Beside one of the pools stood
glowing beast, graceful as waving grass, with one long ho
upon its head.

Mavin ceased in that moment, without thought.

The place from which she came ceased, and the runners
the road. Windlow and Throsset ceased, and the cities of t
world. Night and morning ceased, becoming no more tha
shadow and light. There was water, grass, the unending bler
of foliage in the wind. There was whatever-she-was and th
other, two who were as near to being one as had ever been. Sh
was in another shape when she called from the hill, there fro
the crest where the great black trees bulked like a gatewa
against the stars, called in her beast's voice, a trumpet soun
silvery sweet, receiving the answer like an echo.

He ran to meet her, the sound of his hooves on the gra
making a quick drum beat of joy. Then they were togethe
pressed tight side by side, soft muzzles stroking softer flank
silk on silk, this joy at meeting again no less than the joy the
had had to meet at first, that other time, so long ago. But tha
which-they-were did not think of so-long-ago, nor of th
time-past-when-they-were-not-together, nor of the momen
yet-to-come. Time was not. Before and after was not. Th
naming of names was not, nor the making of connections an
classifications of things. Each thing was its own thing, eac
song in the night, each shadow, each pool, each leaf dancin
upon its twig against the sky.

They simply were.

Sometimes, in the light of morning, when they had walke
slowly across the soft meadows, he would call in that voice sh
knew, and she would flee, racing the very clouds away fro
him, ecstatic at the drum of his hooves following; never so fas
she ran as he could run after; never so fast to flee as he t
pursue. Then they would dance, high on their hind hooves
whirling, manes and tails flourishing in a fine silken fringe t

veil the light, their voices crying fine lusty sounds at the trees, coming into a kind of frenzy at one another, lunging and crying, to settle at last with heaving sides, hearts thudding like the distant thunder.

Sometimes they would lie in the deep grass, chewing the flowers, head to tail as they whisked the glass-winged flies away, talking a kind of stomach talk to one another, content not to move. Then they would rise lazy at midday to stroll to the pools where they would swim, touching the pebbly bottoms with their feet, rolling in the shallows as they tossed great wings of spray against the trees. And at dusk, when the whirling, humming thing came from the stone building at the edge of the rise, they would stand at the gate to let it stroke them and sing in tune with that humming, a song which the birds joined, and the pombi of the forest, and the whirling creature itself.

And sometimes they would run together, outdistancing the wind, fencing the air with their graceful horns, leaping up the piled hills of stone to stand at last like carven things on the highest pinnacles, calling to the clouds which passed.

Sometimes. Time on time.

Until one night the whirling thing came to the place they lay sleeping. It stopped whirling, and sat on the ground beside them and laid one hand upon her head. Her, her head. Her head only. And began to speak.

"This is the garden, Mavin. The garden. Come up, now, out of this place you are in, the wordless place. Come up like a fish from the depths and hear me. This is a garden you are in —the garden, most ancient, adorable, desired. All here is limpid and bright, all details perfect. There are pure animals here, and trees bright with blossom and fruit, streams which sing a soft incessant music and birds which cry bell sounds of joy. There are lawns here, Mavin, green as that light which burns in the heart of legendary stones, and there are other creatures here as well. They lie upon the knolls soft with moss, garlanded with flowers, eating fruits from which a sweet scent rises to the heights.

"Hear me, Mavin. In this land walks also the slaughterer, Death. He comes to an animal or an other and kills it quietly, leaving the body to be eaten by the other beasts and the bones to bleach in the twining grasses. There is no outcry when he comes, for no creature in the garden sees the slaughterer or knows his purpose or anticipates his intent. No one here knows the end of his action, for none in this garden know one moment from another, none know the next moment from the moment at hand. None fear. None are apprehensive for the coming hour, or the morrow, and none hunger or thirst, but all eat and drink and mate and bear in the perfect peace which this garden has always within its borders. Mavin, do you hear me?

"Listen to me, Mavin. There is only peace, tranquility, and simplicity here. And the end of it is Death, Mavin. Only that. Come up out of that dreamless place, Mavin, and think into yourself once more. . . ."

And the peace was destroyed. Not all at once, for she rose and trumpeted her song and ran across the meadow to leave the words behind, but they pursued her, slowing her feet. And when she swam in the pool, she looked into the depths of it and thought of drowning, making a panicky move toward the bank. And when evening came again, she did not lie upon the grasses beside him but stood, head down, musing, unaware that she was changing, Shifting. . . .

The Dervish stood before her, summoning her with a quiet hand. "Come."

A voice which she did not recognize as her own said, "I cannot leave . . . him. . . ."

"For a time," said the Dervish. "Come." And they walked away up the hill toward the low stone building behind the wall.

Inside it was only white space, simple as a box, with a single bench and a cot and a peg upon the wall where clothing could be hung, and one small shelf. The Dervish brought clothing to Mavin, trousers, a shirt, a cloak, a belt and knife. "Put these on."

Mavin looked stupidly down at her nakedness, began to Shift fur to cover herself, was stopped by an imperative "No," from the Dervish. "Put them on." While Mavin was occupied with this, the Dervish took a cup from the shelf, filled it from a flask and gave it to Mavin. "Sit. Drink. Listen to me, Mavin Manyshaped."

"I must go. . . ."

"Listen." The voice was hypnotic, quiet, almost a whisper. "Who is it who lies yonder on the grasses, Mavin Many-shaped?"

"I . . . I don't know. Not a person . . . "

"You know better, Mavin Manyshaped. Who is it who runs trumpeting with you through the glades? Who swims with you in the pools of the garden? Who is your companion?"

"Don't . . . I don't know."

"Come, woman. Do not try me too far. Did you lie to me? You were here before. Eight years ago. You found him here then because I had brought him here. He had enraged the shadow, and it came after him. There is no way to flee from the shadow, only a way to hide—or be hidden. So, I hid him here in shape other than his own, safe for a time, only for a time. . . .

"Then I had to go away. There were things I had to do, great goings on which required my attention. When I returned I found him here and took him away, out of the valley, to a place where it would be safe to change him into his own form. *He would not change.* He could not change. He could not get out of the shape I had given him. So, I brought him back here, thinking to find whatever—whoever it was which had enchanted him more deeply than ever I had intended. I looked here in the valley, but there was no one here. Signs, yes. Tracks so like his own they were made by his twin. But of that beast itself no trace. Whoever had been here was gone.

"And it was you! You who came to him eight years ago! It had to have been a Shifter. Who else? What else!" The Dervish rose, began to spin, to hum, the very walls humming with it as though enraged. After a time it calmed, settled, whispered at her once more. "Mavin Manyshaped, what have you done?"

Mavin sat frozen, like curdled stone, only half aware of what was said, what was meant. Eight years ago Himaggery had disappeared. Eight years ago she, Mavin, had found an idyll in this place. With . . . with . . .

"Himaggery!" she sobbed, at once grieved and joyed, lost and found, the world spinning around her as though it were the Dervish. "Himaggery!"

"Ah." Now the Dervish was quiet. "So you didn't know.

And perhaps you told me the truth when you said you had not been upon the road before? Hmmm. But you had come here, and found him here, and changed, not knowing who he was. Well, having loved you here, my girl, he would not leave the place, would not give up his shape. You did not know it was he. I wonder, somehow, if he knew it was you. Well. Knowing this, perhaps now I can save him."

"Save him for what?" Mavin cried, anguished. "Save him for what, Dervish? Were we not content as we were in your garden? Could you not have left us as we were?"

"Think on that, Shifter-woman. True, I have set some in this garden who will never leave it. But the slaughterer will come, woman. Age will come, and Death. The youthful joy will go, and there will be no joy of the mind to make up for it. Think of it. What would Himaggery have you do, if he could ask?"

Mavin leaned her head in her hands. How long had this gone on? All she wanted to do was return to the garden, leave this simple house and return. If she could not do that? What then? Could she take Himaggery with her?

"Oh, Gamelords, Nameless One. Tell me your name, at least. Let me curse you by name!"

"I am Bartelmy of the Ban, Mavin. It is beneath my Ban that Himaggery was saved from the shadow, within my Ban he has lived these eight years."

"Can we get him out of it?"

"I believe so. I believe you can. Now."

"Well then, Dervish, let us do it. All my body longs only to go back to your garden. Oh, it is a wicked enchantment to make such a longing. See. I am sweating. My nose is running as though I had a fever. Yet inside my head is boiling with questions, with summons, with demands. I would be content to leave it, but it will not leave me. Let us get on with it."

"You are too quick, Shifter. Too quick to Shift, too quick to change, too quick to decide. You came here the second time, and even though I half expected you, you were too quick. Now you would pull Himaggery back into his self without knowing why he was hidden, why that hiding was necessary. No. I will not accept this. Before we try, you and I, to get Himaggery out of the garden I put him in, you must understand why he went there. He was on a search, Shifter. He found at least part of what he was looking for."

"I don't care," Mavin sobbed. "Himaggery is like that. He must understand everything. It doesn't matter to me, not half of what he cares about. If a thing needs to be done, let us do it."

The Dervish made a gesture which froze her as she sat, and the voice which came was terrible in its threat. "I said, too quick, Shifter. I, Bartelmy, will say what you will do. It is for your good, not your harm, and I will not brook your disobedience. You may go willingly or I will take you, but you will see what it was Himaggery saw."

The voice was like ice, and it went into Mavin's heart. There had been something in that voice—something similar to another voice she had heard long before. When? Was it in Ganver's Grave? The Eesty? She drew herself up, slowly, feeling the inner coils of her straighten to attention, readying themselves for flight or attack. Oh, but this was a strange person who confronted her. It was both weaponless and fangless, and yet Mavin shuddered at it, wondering that she could be so dominated in such short time.

It commanded. There was no energy in her to contest its commands, no strength to assert her own independence, her own autonomy. Almost without thought, she knew that this one had a will to match her own—perhaps to exceed her own. Too much had happened, too much was happening for her to consider what might be best to do—so let her do what this Dervish demanded. And if a thing must be done, then better seem to do it willingly than by force. She forced down her quick, instinctively Shifty response to sit silent, waiting.

"Beyond the crest of the hill, Mavin, is a path leading to the south. Walk upon it. You will go three times a rise, three times a fall. On the fourth rise look away to your left. Something will not be there. Seek it out. Examine it. When you have done so, if you still can, return here.

"If you do not draw its attention, it will not follow you." The Dervish began to spin, move, away and out the door of the place, down the meadow and into the trees. Mavin looked among those trees for the silver beast, the lovely beast, the glorious one, her own. A pain too complex to bear broke her

in two, and she gasped as she ran toward the crest of the hill. Gamelords. She would not live to finish this journey.

Once at the crest, it was some time before she could gather her attention to find the southern path. Once on it, her feet followed it of themselves, counting the rises, the falls. She burned inside, an agony, uncaring for the day, the path. The third rise, the third fall. Gasping like a beached fish she came to the last crest and fell to her knees, tears dropping into the dust to make small dirty circles there. At last she stood again and looked off to the left, wondering for the first time how one could see a thing which was not there.

Her glance moved left to right, to left, to right once more, swinging in an arc to that side, only slowly saying to her brain that there was one place in that arc where no message came from the eye. A vacancy. Nothing. She sat upon a log and stared at it. It vanished, filled in with lines of hill and blotches of foliage. She scanned along the hill once more, and it vanished once more. Her throat was suddenly dry, hurtfully dry. There was a streamlet in the valley below, and beyond that stream a hill, and beyond that the upward slope. She struggled down toward the water, catching herself as she slid, somehow not thinking to Shift or unable to do so. At the stream she drank and went on.

As she reached the last hill, she fell to her belly to crawl the last few feet, masking her face with a branch of leafy herb. Below the hill was . . . a road. A side road, a spur leading from the south to end in this place. Upon the road a tower. She thought it was quite tall, but the wavering outlines made it uncertain. If one could get closer . . . It seemed almost to beckon, that wavering. One should get closer.

No! It was as though the Dervish's voice spoke to her where she lay. Himaggery would have gone closer. Being Himaggery, he would have been unable to keep himself away from it. He went down there, saw—something. Something terrible, which did not want to be seen. Something which pursued him.

Then he ran. She could see him in her mind, fleeing down the steep slope, falling, scrambling up to run again, panting, his throat as dry as her own. Run. To the path at the top of the hill, down three times, up three times, growing wearier with each fleeing step, with some horror coming after him. Until he reached the great midnight trees at the entrance to the valley where the Dervish waited. . . .

Whatever had pursued him from this place could not be misled or outrun. So much she had gathered; so much she understood. No. He could hide from this pursuing horror only by giving up everything which made him Himaggery.

So, go no closer, Mavin, she told herself. Watch from here. Find out from here what is there.

Nothing was there.

Nothing boiled at the edges of vision, blurring and twisting like the waves of heat she had seen on long western beaches, making a giddy swirl of every line. For a time there was nothing more than this impression of boiling nothingness to hold her attention, making her feel so dizzy and sick that she gripped the ground beneath her, digging her nails deep into gravelly soil which seemed to tilt and sway. Then, when time passed and her eyes became accustomed to the unfocused roiling, she saw there was substance—if not substance, then color —to whatever shifted and boiled. It was not another hue. Greens were not bluer or yellower, browns not more red or ocher. It was, instead, as though all color was grayed, darkened, becoming mere hint and allusion to itself, a ghostly code for the shades and tints of the world. This allusive grayness piled upon the roadway, flickered around the outlines of the tower she believed she saw, coalescing into writhing mounds, fracturing into fluttering flakes.

Breaking away, one such flake flew upward toward her, coming to rest upon the littered slope. Behind it as it flew the trees lost their gold-green vitality to appear as a brooding lace of bones against the sky; at first an entire copse, then a narrower patch, then a thin belt of gray which striped the trees. As it came to rest, the shadow became wider once more, the copse behind it showing gray and grim. After a chilly time, her mind translated this into a reality, a thing seen if only in effect; something leaf-shaped, thin when seen edge on but broad in its other dimensions, something which could lift or fly and was, perhaps, like those other flakes crawling in nightmare drifts upon the roadway.

Shadows. Shadows which moved of themselves. She put her face into her hands and lay there silently, unable to look at them because of the vertiginous dizzyness they caused. She was helpless until the nausea passed, leaving a shaky weakness in its place. Then she could breathe again, and she opened her eyes to watch, not daring to move.

There were birds nesting in the trees behind her. She heard them scolding, saw their shadows dash across the ground as they sought bits of litter and grass. One of them darted near her face. It hopped toward a bunch of grasses on which the shadow flake lay, gathering dried strands as it went. There was plenty of grass outside the shadow. The bird half turned, as though to go the other way, but a breeze moved the grasses. Within the shadow, they beckoned. The bird turned and hopped into the shadowed space. The grasses dropped from its beak. It squatted, wings out, beak open, then turned its head with horrid deliberation to peck at one wing as though it attacked some itching parasite.

All was silent. Mavin lay without breathing, prone, almost not thinking. Before her on the slope in the patch of shadow a bird pecked at its wing, pecked, pecked.

After a time the shadow lifted lazily, hovering as it turned, becoming a blot, a line, a blot once more as it rejoined the clotted shadow at the tower. Behind it on the slope a bird stopped pecking. With a pitiable sound it stumbled away from its own wing which lay behind it, severed.

Mavin drew upon the power of the place without thinking. She Shifted one hand into a lengthy tentacle, reached out for the bird and snapped its neck quickly to stop the thin cry of uncomprehending pain. The piled shadows heaved monstrously, as though someone had spoken a word they listened for. They had noticed something—the draw of power, her movement, the bird's death. She could not watch any longer. Head down, she wriggled back the way she had come.

When she had returned to the road, she saw shadows there as well, one or two upon the verges, a few moving across the sky from tree to tree. At the top of each rise were a few, and in each hollow. As she approached the great midnight trees at the entrance to the valley, she saw others there, more, enough to shimmer the edges of the guardian trees in an uneasy dance. Between them stood the Dervish.

"You have seen." It was not a question. It was a statement

of fact. Mavin knew what she had seen showed in her face; she could imagine the look of it. Ashamed. Terrorized.

"I have seen something," she croaked. "I do see. They lie in the trees around us."

"I know," the Dervish replied. "In usual times, they lie only upon the tower as they have done for centuries, hiding it from mortal eyes, hiding the bell within. I have seen them, as have others before me. But Himaggery was not content merely to see. He attempted to penetrate, to get into the tower."

"How is that possible?"

"To a Wizard, anything is possible," the Dervish said with more than a hint of scorn. "Or so they lead themselves to believe."

"If you think so little of Wizards, why did you save him from the shadows at all?" Mavin asked this with what little anger she could muster.

"I counted it my fault he went there. He asked about the tower and I answered, not realizing his arrogance. I did not warn. Therefore this disturbance was my responsibility, Shifter. At least for that time. Now it is one I will pass on to you, for it is you who thwarted my releasing him. You will take him away with you. His presence, and yours, disturb my work."

"If you'll put him into his own form," agreed Mavin, not caring at the moment what the Dervish's work might be. "Though he may immediately try to go back to the tower and finish whatever it was he started...."

The Dervish hummed a knifelike sound which brought Mavin to her knees, gasping. "Not in his own form! And he will not go back to that tower! How far do you think these will let him go in his own form?" The Dervish gestured at the shadows, making a sickening swooping motion with both arms, then clutching them tight and swaying. "They would have him tight-wrapped in moments. No. It must be far and far from here, Mavin Manyshaped, that he is brought out of that shape. Come!"

There were no shadows in the valley, at least none that Mavin could see. There was a silvery beast waiting beside the flowery pools, and she fought the instinctive surge toward him, the flux of her own flesh inside its skin. There was a pombi there as well, huge and solemn beside the low wall, leaning against it, an expression of lugubrious patience upon its furry face.

"Come out, Arkhur," commanded the Dervish.

The pombi stood on its hind legs, stretched, faded to stand before Mavin as a sad-faced, old youngster dressed in tattered garments. Mavin gasped. It was the face she had seen at the Lake of Faces, the other which had spoken of Bartelmy's Ban. So here was Chamferton's brother, wearily obedient to this Dervish.

"Go back, Arkhur," said the Dervish.

The youth dropped to all fours and became a pombi once more.

"I didn't know anyone could do that," grated Mavin. "Except Shifters, and then only to themselves."

"No one can, except Shifters, and only to themselves. He only believes he is a pombi. You believe it because he believes it. He believes it because I believe it. Even the shadows believe—no, say rather the shadows do not find in him that pattern they seek. When Himaggery went to the tower, he found this one nearby, enchanted, perhaps, or drugged, or both. When Himaggery fled, he carried this one out with him, though he would have been wiser to go faster and less encumbered. I hid him as I hid Himaggery, though it is probable it was not as necessary. Now both must go. Those you meet upon the road will believe he is a pombi.

"So, too, with the other. He believes he is the fabulous beast he appears to be to others. You believe it also. All others will believe it. The shadows will not sense in him the pattern they seek. But you must go far from here, very far, Mavin Manyshaped. No trifling distance will do. You must be several days' journey from your last view of the shadows before you bring him out into himself once more. Do it as I did. Call his name; tell him to come out. *Make him hear you*, and he will come out."

"A place far from here." Mavin staggered, too weary to stand. "Far from here."

"A place well beyond the last shadow, a place where no shadow is," the Dervish agreed.

She took up a halter which was hanging upon the gate, and

wondered in passing whether it was real or whether she only believed she saw it. Whichever it might have been, the fabulous beast believed he felt it, for he called a trumpet sound of muted grief as they went up the road past the guardian trees, the pombi shambling behind them.

Chapter 5

They could not go far enough. Mavin stumbled as she led the beast, dragged her feet step on step, looking up to see shadows in every tree they passed beneath, on every line of hill, in every nostril of earth. Still, she went on until she knew she could go no farther, then tethered the beast to a tree and coaxed him to lie down as a pillow for her head. The pombi lay beside them without being coaxed, and warmed by the furry solidity she rested. The smooth body beneath her cheek breathed and breathed. She forced herself not to respond to that gentle movement, though she passionately desired to lie tight against that body and abandon herself to the closeness, the warmth. Something in the beast responded to her, and he turned to bring her body closer, touching the soft flesh of her neck with a muzzle as soft. She forced herself away, trying to find a position which would not so stir her feelings, found one of sheer weariness at last. Thus they slept, moving uneasily from time to time as night advanced, and it was in the dark of early morning that she woke to begin the trek once more.

The thought of food began to obsess her. She did not know what the beast could eat. She remembered eating grass when she had been his mate, but she had actually Shifted into a form which could eat grass. What did Himaggery eat in this strange shape he thought he bore? Did belief extend to such matters as teeth and guts? Could she feed such a beast on grasses which would not keep the man alive? The pombi did not wait upon her consideration. He shambled off into the forest and returned with a bunwit dangling from his jaws, munching on it with every appearance of satisfaction. Soon after, they passed a rainhat bush. Mavin peeled a ripe fruit and offered it from her hand. The beast took it with soft lips and a snuffle of pleasure. Had it not been for the shadows clustered around them, she would have felt pleased.

"I cannot call you . . . Himaggery," she whispered, giving no voice to the name itself. "Not even to myself. To do so starts something within me I cannot hold. And I may not think of you as I did when I was your mate within the valley, for to do so melts my flesh, beast. So. What shall I call you?" She considered this while they walked a league or so, the pombi licking bunwit blood from his bib of white hair, she feeding the other two of them on fruit and succulent fronds of young fern which thrust their tight coils up among the purple spikes of Healer's balm. Only the rainhat bush bore fruit so early, and she gave some thought to the monotony of the beast's diet if, indeed, it could not eat grass or graze upon the young leaves.

"I will call you Fon," she said at last. "For you were Fon when we met. Or I will call you Singlehorn."

The beast stopped, staring about himself as though in confusion, and she knew her words had reached some inner self which was deeply buried.

"Fon," she said in pity. "It's all right. It's all right, my Singlehorn."

It was not all right. The shadows had only multiplied as they went, as though attracted by some ripe stink of passion or pain. Something in the relationship among the three of them, perhaps, or between any two of them. Something, perhaps, which sought to surface in either Arkhur or . . . Fon. Something, perhaps, which sought expression in herself. She thought of the bird which had severed its own wing, wondering what had motivated the shadow to cause such a thing, or whether any creature, once it had invaded the shadow, would have acted so automatically. Yet Himaggery had sought to inade the tower and had somehow escaped.

The bird had simply gone into the shadow.

How had Himaggery gone?

The shadows had not sought the bird. Or had they?

The shadows were seeking something now. Seeking, follow-
ng, but not attacking. She wondered at their passivity, know-
ng they could attack if they would. Their failure to do so was
more frightening than the actuality, making heart labor and
breath caw through a dry throat without purpose. Running
would not help. Conversation would make her feel less lonely,
but there was no one present who could answer her. Even her
words were dangerous, for either of the beasts beside her
might rise to an unintentional inflection, an unmeant phrase,
ise into that pattern which the shadows sought.

So, in a forced silence, for the first time since leaving the
valley, she began to consider where they were going. Somewhere without shadows. And where might such a place be
found?

"We need a Wizard," she whispered to herself. "One walks
at my back, and I cannot use him. Chamferton is far to the
east of us. Besides, I cannot like him, dare not trust him. So.
Perhaps instead of a Wizard, I need . . . a Seer. To find the
shadowless place. And who would be more interested than
Windlow, Fon-beast, eh? Far and far from here, down the
whole length of the land to the mountainous places of Tarnoch. Still, I could rely upon him. And once there—once there
we could rest."

Even though the shadows did not attack, they were present.
Weariness followed upon that fact, a weightiness of spirit, a
heaviness of heart and foot and hand so that mere bodies
became burdens. Mavin wondered dully if she could Shift into
something which would be less susceptible to this lassitude and
was warned by some inner voice to stay as she was, not to
change, not to draw upon any power from the earth or air, for
it was such a draw upon the power of the place which had
stirred the shadows in her presence once before.

"As we are, then," she sighed. "As we are, companions.
One foot before another, and yet again, forever. Gamelords,
but we have come a wearying way."

They had not come far and she knew it. They had gone up

and down a half-dozen small hills, tending always south, toward the road of tingling stones where the blind runners had been. She did not know why she had set out with that destination in mind except that it was a real place, a measurable distance from other places she knew, not so far that it seemed unattainable even to a group as weary as this one.

One rise and then another. One hollow and then another. Trees blotted dark on a line of hill. Rocks twisted into devil faces; foliage in the likeness of monsters. Clouds which moved faster in the light wind than they three moved upon the earth. Each measure a measure of a league's effort to cross a quarter of it. Until at last they came to a final rise and saw the pale line of the road stretching across its feet.

The day had dawned without sun and moved to noon in half light. They could go no further, but she led them on until the road itself was beneath their feet. Once there, they dropped into a well of sleep as sudden as a clap of thunder. No shadow moved on this road. No shadow moved near this road. Pale it stretched from east to west, the stones of it cracked into myriad hairline fissures in which fernlets grew, and buttons of fungus, their minute parasols shedding a tiny fog of spores upon the still air. Mavin lay upon them like a felled sapling, all asprawl, loose and lost upon the stones, the beasts beside her. In their sleep they seemed to flatten as though the stones absorbed them, drew them down, and when they woke at last they lay long, half conscious, drawing their flesh back up into themselves.

It was music which had wakened them, far off and half heard on a fitful wind, but music nonetheless. A thud of great drum; a snarl of small drum; blare and tootle, rattle and clash, louder as it continued, obviously nearing. There were no shadows nearby though Mavin saw flutters against a distant copse. She dragged herself up, tugging the beasts into the trees at the side of the road. They stood behind leafy branches, still half asleep, waiting for what would come.

What came was a blare of trumpets, a pompety-pom of drums, three great crashes of cymbals, thrangggg, thranggg, thranggg, then a whole trembling thunder of music over the rise to the east. They saw the plumes first, red and violet, purple and azure, tall and waving like blown grass. The plumes were upon black helmets, glossy as beetles, small and tight to the heads of the musicians who came with their cheeks puffed out and their eyes straight ahead, following one who marched before them raising and lowering his tall, feathered staff to set the time of the music. Mavin felt the Fon-beast's horn in the small of her back, up and down, up and down, marching in time to the music. Looking down, she saw pombi feet, Fon feet, and Mavin feet all in movement, pom, pom, pom, pom, as the bright music tootled and bammed around them.

The musicians were dressed in tight white garments with colorful fabric wrapped about them to make bright kilts from their waists to below their knees, reflecting the hues of the plumes as they swished and swung, left-right, left-right. Polished black boots thumped upon the stones; the musicians moved on. Behind came the children, ranks and files of them, some with small instruments of their own, and behind the children the wagons, horses as brightly plumed as the musicians were, the elderly drivers sitting tall as the animals kept step, legs lifted high in a prance.

She could see no shadows anywhere near, not upon the road nor within the forest, perhaps not within sound of the music. Mavin moved onto the roadway behind the last of the wagons. From the back of it, an apple-cheeked old woman nodded at them with a smile of surprise, tossing out a biscuit which the Fon caught between his teeth. Mavin got the next one and the pombi the third, throwing it high to catch it on the next step, marching as it chewed in the same high, poised trot the wagon horses displayed.

"Are you Circus?" cried the old woman from a toothless mouth. "Haven't seen Circus in a lifetime!"

Mavin had no idea what she meant, but she smiled and nodded, the Singlehorn pranced, and Arkhur-pombi rose to his hind legs in a grave two-step. So they went, on and on, keeping step to the drums even when the other instruments stopped tweedling and flourishing for a time. The sun dropped lower in their faces, and lower yet, until only a glow remained high among the clouds, pink as blossoms.

Then the whistle, shreeee, shreee; whompity-womp, bang, bang. Everything stopped.

A busy murmur, like a hive of bees. Shouts, cries, animals unhitched and led to the grassy verges of the road. Fires started almost upon the road itself, and cookpots hung above them. Steam and smoke, and a crowd of curious children gathering around the Fon-beast and Arkhur-pombi, not coming near, but not fearful either, full of murmurs and questions.

"Are they trained, Miss? Can you make them do tricks? Can you ride them? Would they let me ride them? Are you Circus?"

"What," she asked at last, "is Circus?"

"Animals," cried one. To which others cried objection, "No, it's jugglers." "Clowns." "Acrobats, Nana-bat says." "It's marvels, that's what."

An older child approached, obviously one to whom the welfare of these had been assigned, for he wore a worried expression which looked perpetual and shook his head at the children in a much practiced way. "Why are you annoying the travelers? One would think you'd never seen an animal trainer before. We saw one just last season, when we left the jungle cities."

"Not with animals like this, Hirv." "Those were only fusti gars, Hirv." "Nobody ever told me you could train pombis, Hirv." "Hirv, what's the one with the horn. Ask her, will you Hirv."

"That beast is a Singlehorn," Mavin replied in an ingratiating tone. "The pombi was raised by humans since it was a cub." Which is true enough, she told herself. Arkhur must have been raised by someone. "I am not their trainer. I am merely taking them south to their owner." She had thought this out fairly carefully, not wanting to be asked to have the beasts do tricks. "If it would not disturb you, we would like to go along behind you for a time. Your music makes the leagues shorter." And she provided another ingratiating expression to put herself in their good graces. The children seemed inclined to accept her, but the one who was approaching next might be harder to convince.

He was the music master, he of the tall, plumed staff and the silver whistle. He thrust through the children, planted the staff on the pave and looked them over carefully before turning to the child-minder. "What does she want?"

"Only to follow along, Bandmaster. She says it makes the leagues shorter."

The Bandmaster allowed himself a chilly smile. "Of course it does. The Band swallows up the leagues as though it had wings. Music bears us up and carries us forward. In every land in every generation."

The children had evidently heard this before, for there was tittering among them; and one, braver than the rest, puffed himself up in infant mockery, pumping a leafy branch as though he led the marching.

"What is your name?" the Bandmaster demanded.

"Mavin," she said, making a gestured bow. "With two beasts to deliver to the southland."

"I assume they are not dangerous? We need not fear for our children?"

Mavin thought of the murdered bunwit and looked doubtfully at Arkhur-pombi, who returned the gaze innocently, tongue licking at its breast hairs, still slightly stained with bunwit blood. "I will keep it near me, Bandmaster. Can you tell me where you have come from? I have traveled up and down this land for twenty years, and I have not run across your like before."

The Bandmaster smiled a superior smile, waving his hand to an elder who lingered to one side, arms clutched tight around a bundle of books. "Where have we been in twenty years, Byram? The Miss wishes to know."

The oldster sank to his haunches, placing the bundle on the ground to remove one tome and leaf through it, counting as he leafed back, stopping at last to cry in a reedy voice, "Twenty years ago we were on the shores of the Glistening Sea nearby to Levilan. From there we went north along the shore road to the sea cities of Omaph and Peeri and the northern bays of Smeen. And from there," leafing forward in his book, "to the Citadel of Jallywig in the land of the dancing fish, thence north once more along Boughbound Forest to the glades of Shivermore and Creep and thence south to the jungle roads of the Great Maze. Oh, we were on the roads of the Great Maze ten years, Miss, and glad to see the end of them at last in the jungle cities of Luxuri and Bloome. And from there south across the Dorbor Range onto the old road where we are now. We have played the repertoire forty times through in twenty years. . . ."

"How long have you been doing this?" she asked. "Traveling around this way?"

"How long have we been *marching*," corrected the Bandmaster. "Why, since the beginning, of course. Since disembarkation or shortly thereafter. At first, so it is written, there were few roads and long, Miss, but as we go they ramify. Ah, yes, they ramify. Used to be in time past, so it is written, we could make the circuit in five years or so. Now it takes us seventy. In time, I suppose, there will be children born who will never live to see their birthplace come up along the road again. Jackabib, there, with his leafy bough pretending to mock the Bandmaster, why, it may be he will never see the city of Bloome again."

Jackabib did not seem distressed by this thought. He only flushed a little and ran off into the trees where he peeked at them from among the leaves like a squirrel.

"Well then, I would not have seen you," agreed Mavin. "You have not been this way in my lifetime. I am mighty glad you came this way now, however, for it is a sight I will always remember." And a sound, she thought, aware of the ache in her legs. The sound had carried them step on step, and never a sign of weariness or hurt until the music stopped. "This pombi is pretty good as a hunter, as am I. May we contribute meat for the pot?"

This was agreed to with good cheer, so she led Arkhur beast into the trees and set him on the trail. She poised, then, ready to Shift herself into hunting fustigar shape, only to stop, listening, for it seemed she heard a deep, solemn humming in the trees. The sound faded. She took a deep breath, began the Shift, then heard it once more. The voice came on the little wind like a sigh. "Do not Shift, Mavin. Stay as you are. You risk much if you Shift, the shadows not least."

When it had spoken, she was not sure she had heard it. When she readied herself once more, however, she knew she had heard it, for her flesh twinged away from the idea of *Shift* as though it had been burned.

"Well then," she said to herself, not ready yet to be worried at this. "I will do as the children of Danderbat Keep were taught to do. I will set snares."

Arkhur-pombi returned to her from time to time with his prey, like a cat bringing marshmice to the door. Each time Mavin patted him and took the proferred bunwit with expressions of joy, as though he had indeed been some young hunting beast she sought to train. She laughed at herself, yet went on doing it. Her snares, set across burrow runways, were also useful; and they returned to the wagons some hours later, Mavin's arms laden with furry forms, even after feeding two of them to Arkhur to assure the safety of the children.

She found the people of the band occupied with a myriad orderly duties, cooking, cleaning their musician dresses, polishing boots and helmets, copying strange symbols by firelight on squares of parchment which they told her conveyed the music they played. Mavin had not seen written music before, and she marveled at it, as strange and exotic a thing as she could remember ever having seen. Others of them gathered food from the forest by torchlight, rainhat berries, fern fronds, fungus to be sliced and dried before the fires. "When we play in the cities," she was told, "we are given coin, and we use that coin to fill the meal barrels and the meat safes. Between times, we must live upon the land."

The Fon-beast, tethered to a tree, was suffering himself to be petted and decked with flowers by a tribe of children. Mavin offered fruit and bread from her hand, only to be copied by all the young ones. So she could leave the Singlehorn without guilt in their tender hands and sit by other fires to hear what these people knew. She ended the evening telling stories of lands across the sea, of giant chasms and bridge-people who lived below the light, and stickies—one of whom, at least, probably remembered the days of disembarkation. "His name is Mercald-Myrtilon," she said. "And he has memories in him of that time a thousand years long past." There was much expression of interest and wonder at this, and the Bandmaster even began to talk of taking a ship to that farther shore to march there, until Mavin told him there were no roads at all.

After which she slept beside her beasts along with half a dozen children who had fallen asleep while petting or feeding one or both. When they woke, it was a brighter world than on any recent morning.

"Come, Arkhur-pombi," she teased the beast up and into motion. "There are no shadows near this road, and I must risk us both to learn something sensible." She took him off into the trees, not far, watching all the time for that telltale darkening of foliage or sky, seeing nothing but the honest shadows cast by the sun. There in a sweet clearing full of unrolling ferns she told him in the closest approximation of the Dervish's voice, "Arkhur, come out!"

It was some time before he did, rising on his hind legs, dropping again, circling uneasily, then at last seeming to set his mind to it. The figure which materialized out of the pombi's shape was no more impressive than before. It still had that young-old expression of apologetic intransigence, a face which said, "I know you all think this a stupid idea, and perhaps I do also, but I must get on with it." When he was fully before her, he seemed to have no idea what to do with his hands, but stood waving them aimlessly, as though brushing flies.

"You are Arkhur?" she asked in a gentle voice, not wanting to startle him. "Younger brother of the High Wizard Chamferton?"

She might as well have struck him with a whip. His eyes flashed; his back straightened; the hands came down before him in a gesture of firm negation.

"I am Arkhur," he said in a furious tenor. "I *am* the High Wizard Chamferton, younger brother of a foul Invigilator who despised his Talent and sought to usurp mine!"

"Ahh," she breathed. "So that was it. And how came you to this pass, Arkhur—or should I call you High Wizard, or sir? I called your brother by your name, I'm afraid, but it doesn't surprise me to learn the truth. He had a slyness about him."

"I trusted him," the pombi-man growled, so suddenly angry he was almost incoherent. Mavin had to struggle to understand him as he spat and gargled. "I trusted his pleas for understanding and rest. He told me he was an old man. Beyond scheming anymore, he said. Beyond treachery. Want-

ing only warm fires and warm food, cool wine and quiet sur-
roundings. And so I took him in. And he stayed, learned,
Read me when I least expected it, then drugged me deep and
sent me to be Harpy-dropped where the shadows dance. Fool!
Oh, much will I treasure vengeance against him, woman. But
well will I repay the Gamesmen who brought me away from
the shadows and the tower." He seemed to savor this for the
moment, then demanded:

"Where is he?"

Mavin assumed he meant Himaggery. She shook her head.
"He is near, but worse off than you, Wizard. Now, before
you say anything more, tell me a thing. The Dervish who hid
you told me to bring you out of the pombi shape '*where no
shadow was.*' Well, there is no shadow here, but I doubt not
they are somewhere perhaps within sight of us. Are you in
danger in your shape? And if so, shall I return you to beastli-
ness?"

At first the High Wizard Chamferton understood none of
this and it took considerable time for Mavin to explain it. By
the time he had climbed a tree to see for himself where
shadows lay upon the line of hills, smells of breakfast were
wafting from the fires along the road, and they were both
hungry.

"My brother used a certain drug on me, Mavin. He knows
little enough of his own Talent, and even less of mine, or he
would have realized that in that drugged state, the shadows
would pay me no more attention than they might pay a block
of wood. Though I could see them and even consider them in a
dreamy way, I had no more volition than a chopping block.
No. They did not care about me and will not be attracted to
me. I am certain of that."

"Certain enough to risk our lives?" she persisted.

He nodded, again solemn. "Certain."

"Well, that's something the Dervish didn't know." This
made Mavin cheerful for some reason. It was good to think
that there were some things a Dervish might not know. "Well
then, how do I explain the loss of the pombi?"

"Don't explain it. Put me back as I was, woman, and let us
part from these good people amiably. Perhaps in time we will
want their friendship. Then, when we have separated from

them, you can bring me out again. Next time it will not be such a task, for I will set myself to remember who I am, even in pombi shape."

Mavin, well aware of the lure of forgetfulness which came with any beast shape, did not totally believe this optimistic statement but was content to try it. "Go back, Arkhur," she said, needing to say it only once. They emerged from the trees to the welcoming bugle of the Singlehorn and in time for breakfast.

"Have you a map of the way you are going?" she asked the old man, Byram, who seemed to be totally responsible for all matters of record. "Perhaps I might rejoin your party farther on?"

He sniffled, scuffled, laid the map out on a wagon's hinged side and pointed out to her the way they would go.

"Well, here's the way of it, girl. Last time we were by here, I was a youngun. 'Prentice to the manager before me, just as he was to the one before him clear back to disembarkation. He took the notes and went over 'em with me, and I took 'em down myself, just to have another copy—he used to say that a lot: 'one copy's a fool's copy,' meaning if you lost the one, where'd you be? Eh? Well, so I always had my own copy made from then on. Now, though, after fifty years, try and read it! So look here. It goes from where we are on west, and west, bumpety-bump, all through these whachacallems forests. . . ."

"Shadowmarches," offered Mavin. "This whole area west of the Dorbor Mountains and east of the sea, north of the Cagihiggy Creek cliffs, all the way to the jungles."

"Sha-dow-mar-ches," he wrote laboriously, spelling it out. "Well now, that's good to know. So, westward, westward for a long straight way, then we come to the coast and turn away down south. No road north from there, just trails. At least fifty years ago was just trails. Maybe won't be any road south either, now, but we can usually find flat enough to march on.

"Anyhow, the road goes south and south until it comes to this long spit of land heading right out into the sea, down the west side of this great bay, almost an inland sea. Well, the road goes along south. East across the bay you can see a town, here, at the river mouth. What d'ya call that?"

"Ummm," said Mavin, puzzling out the map. "That's Hawsport."

"Right! See, those little letters right there. That's what they say. Hawsport. So you know it's been there a while, don't you? Well, we go on until we're well south of Hawsport, then the spit of land turns east a little, coming closer to the mainland, closer and closer until it gets to a bridge."

"I don't think there's a bridge there," said Mavin. "Not that I remember." She tried to summon bird memories of the coast as seen from above, as she had crossed it again and again in the long years' search for Handbright. No bridge. Certainly not one of the length the old man's map called for.

"Now then, isn't that what I said to the Bandmaster! I said, likely that bridge's gone, I said. There was a storm not long after we were here before that would have been a horror and a disaster to any bridge ever built. Even if it isn't gone, likely it's in a state of sorrowful disrepair. Oh, the bridges we've gone over that trembled to our step, girl, let me tell you, it's no joke when a band must break step to keep a bridge from collapsing. And the ones we've not dared tread on and have had to go around, ford the stream, march along the river to a better place. Bridges! They're the bane of my life."

"I truly don't think there's one there," she repeated. "What will you do if there isn't?"

"Well that's not my problem," he said, folding the map with small, precise gestures. "I've told Bandmaster, told him in front of half the horn section just this morning, and he paid me no mind. So we get there and no bridge? Well, that's his problem, not mine."

"You'll have to go back?" she asked.

"Likely. And wouldn't that make him look silly." The old man giggled into his hands in a childlike way, then harumphed himself into a more dignified expression. "If you don't find us on the shore, Mavin, you look for us across the great bay. Likely we'll be there, waiting for boats!"

Mavin had to be satisfied with this. She felt she could take twenty days or more and still meet them somewhere on the road, across the bay or this side of it, safe from shadows. Or so she told herself to comfort the cold sorrow with which she left them. Perhaps she would only bring Arkhur into his own shape and let him go east alone. Perhaps, she told herself, watching him shamble along behind the wagons, that solemn expression upon his face, as though he considered all the troubles of the world.

After the noon meal she left the Band, turning aside on a well traveled track as though such a destination had been intended from the beginning. When the Band had tootled itself away into the west, no more than a small cloud of dust upon the horizon, she stood upon the ancient pave and said, "Arkhur, come out." This time he was less hesitant, and he did remember himself—which somewhat increased her respect for Wizards, or at least for this one—so that their way east could begin immediately. Only Singlehorn stood behind them, crying into the west as though he could not bear the music to be gone. Mavin had to tug him smartly by the halter before he moved, and even then it was with his head down, his horn making worm trails of gloom in the dust.

"There is the one who saved you, Arkhur. We are not far enough from the shadows to restore him to his own shape, but his name," she whispered, "is Himaggery, and you may choose to remember it. You will want to return to your own demesne. There is probably little I could do to help you there, and since it is not our affair, we will go on south."

"It is not your affair," he agreed in a troubled voice, "if you are sure my brother has not your Face at the Lake of Faces, yours nor Himaggery's. I need not search the place to be sure he has mine!"

"He does have Himaggery's," she confessed. "Though he said it did not hurt those from whom he took them. No more than a pin prick, he said."

"No more than a pin prick at the time, no more than a year's life lost each time he questions the Face thereafter. He need only send evil Pantiquod or her daughter Foulitter, to question a Face some forty or fifty days running, and the life of even a youngish person would be gone. I am sure he questions my Face from time to time, to no purpose so long as I was in the Dervish's valley. What would it have said?"

The question had been rhetorical, but Mavin answered it. "It said the same as Himaggery's did; that you were under Bartelmy's Ban."

He thought deeply, hands covering his eyes as he concentrated upon this information. "Well, I think it likely that such an answer did not shorten my life nor Himaggery's. But my brother Dourso will not cease questioning. He may be there now, or tomorrow, asking of my Face. And when he hears I am no longer under—what was it you said?—Bartelmy's Ban, will he not strip me of what life I have left as soon as he may? And he will not neglect to take yours, Mavin, and Himaggery's as well. Do not ask me why, for I do not know, but it is no coincidence that all three of us came from Chamferton's aerie to the Shadow Tower." He gloomed over this, seeking a solution. "No. We must go quickly to the Lake of Faces, you as well as I, for either one of us alone might be unable to complete the task. Run as we may, are we not six days, eight days from the Lake of Faces? More perhaps?"

"You, perhaps," she said. "Not I." Even if she could not Shift, dare not Shift, for some reason only the Dervish understood, she could lengthen her legs and her stride. That was not truly Shifting. It was only a minor modification. "It is likely he has my Face as well. I slept deeply when I was there, too deeply, now I think of it. Perhaps he took my Face. . . ."

"I think it probable," Arkhur said. "More than probable. In my day I had a dozen Faces there, no more, all of them of evil men or women whose lives are a burden to the world. Even so, I questioned them seldom and only in great need. Not so my brother! I doubt not he has filled the Lake with them, and the forest as well." Seeing Mavin's expression, he nodded, confirmed in his belief. "Well then, we must move as quickly as we can. You must go there swiftly, Mavin. Take our masks down from the posts on which they hang and press them deep into the Lake. They will dissolve. Once gone, they are no danger."

"Can you run faster as a pombi?" she asked, wondering whether he would know.

"No faster than when I am not," he said, "except that I may run safer."

"Will you bring Singlehorn as quickly as you can? I can go faster without either of you. It will perhaps save a day or two—a year or two. . . ."

The High Wizard Chamferton looked at her with serious

eyes, and Mavin knew she could trust him with her own life or any other she could put in his keeping, to the limit of his ability. She nodded at him. "I will make a trail for you to follow. Watch for signs along the road." Then she spoke as the Dervish had done once more. "Go back, Arkhur."

She ran away to the east without looking behind her, lengthening her legs as she went. There were still no shadows near nor on the road. It stretched away east, straight and clear, edged by long, ordinary sun shadows from the west, seeming almost newly built in that light. She fled away, stride on stride, leaving them behind, hearing the shuffle of pombi feet and the quick tap of Singlehorn hooves fade into the silence of the afternoon.

Chapter 6

She had not gone far before discovering that it was one thing to run long distances when one could Shift into a runner —whether fustigar shape or some other long-legged thing— and quite another thing when one must run on one's own two legs, even when they were lengthened and strengthened a bit for the job. The road was hard and jarring. She stepped off it to run on the grassy verge, seeing the shadows lying under the trees, wondering if they were of that same evil breed she had seen around the tower, knowing they were only a flutter away from her if they chose to move. The fact that they did not made them no less horrible.

She fell into a rhythm of movement, a counting of strides, one hundred then a hundred more then a hundred more. It seemed to her that she felt weariness more quickly than she had done on other similar occasions. Was it age? Was it only having to run in her own shape? Was it the fact that she ran eastward toward the Harpies once more, toward that paralyzing fascination she had felt once and dreaded to feel again? Was it the presence of the shadows? Was it that other thing— whatever it was—which prevented her Shifting? And what was that other thing? A mystery. Inside herself or outside?

Eighty-five, eighty-six, eighty-seven . . .

It isn't the Dervish who speaks to me, telling me not to Shift, she told herself. Even though I hear that strange Dervishy humming all around, it isn't the Dervish. If the Dervish had known a reason I should not Shift, the Dervish would have said so, just as it said too many other things.

Besides, when she had pulled power there on the hillside above the shadowed tower, the chill had attracted their attention, or it had seemed to do so. So it might be her own dream-mind telling her to be careful, telling her things her awake-mind was too busy to notice. Too busy to notice. As, for example, how relieved she was to have left the Fon-beast behind. . . .

"That's not true!" she tried to tell herself. "That's nonsense."

The denial was not convincing. It *was* true; she was relieved to have left him behind. There was too much feeling connected with his presence, a kind of loving agony which pulled first one way then another, making her conscious of her body all the time. It was easier not to worry about that, easier to be one's own self for a time.

"Selfish," she admonished herself. "Selfish, just as Huld and Huldra were, thinking only of themselves."

"Nonsense." Some internal monitor objected to this. "You have lived for thirty-five years on your own, mostly alone, not having to worry about another person every day, every hour. Thirty-five years sets habits in place, Mavin. It is only that this new responsibility disturbs your sense of the usual, that's all."

But it was not all. If that had been all she could have left the Fon-beast at any time for any reason, and so long as he was cared for, she should have felt no guilt. If that had been all, it would not have mattered who cared for him. But as it was, she knew she would not leave the Fon-beast unless it were necessary to save his life. He was now her responsibility. Set into her care. Given to her. Foisted upon her. She could no more turn her back on that than she could have turned her back on Handbright's children. "But I did not agree to that," she said to herself in a pleading voice. "I did not agree to that at all."

Seventy-one, seventy-two, seventy-three . . .

"You agreed to meet him. Of such strange foistings are meetings made."

She did not know where these voices came from, familiar voices, sometimes older, sometimes younger than her own. They had always spoken to her at odd moments, calling her to account for her actions—usually when it was far too late to do anything about them. "Ghosts," she suggested to herself. "My mother's ghost? Ghosts of all the Danderbat women, dead and gone." It was an unprofitable consideration which distracted her attention from covering the leagues east. She tried to think of something else, to concentrate upon counting her strides.

One hundred, and a hundred more, and a hundred more. . .

Responsibility. Who had taught her the word? Handbright, of course. "Mavin, it is your responsibility to take the plates down to the kitchen. Mavin, you are responsible for Mertyn. Don't let him out of your sight. Mavin, you must acquire a sense of responsibility. . . ."

What was responsibility after all but a kind of foisting? Laying a burden on someone without considering whether that person could bear it or wanted to bear it. Dividing up the necessaries among the available hands to do it, though always exempting certain persons from any responsibility at all. Oh, that was true. Some were never told they must be responsible. Boy-children in Danderbat Keep, for example.

So it was some went through life doing as they chose without any responsibility or only with those responsibilities they chose for themselves. Others had it laid upon them at every turn. So Handbright had tried to lay responsibility upon Mavin, who had evaded it, run from it, denied it. She had not felt guilty about that in the past. Why then did she feel guilt because she relished being on her own again, away from the thin leather strap which tied her to the Fon-beast, linking her to him by a halter of protection and guidance, a determination to bring him to himself safely—one hoped—at last. And it was not really the Dervish who had laid it on her; she had laid it on herself—laid it on with that promise twenty years ago.

"Every promise is like that," she whispered to herself as she stopped counting strides for a moment. "Every promise has arms and legs and tentacles reaching off into other things and other places and other times, strange bumps and protrusions you don't see when you make the promise. Then you find you've taken up some great, lumpty thing you never knew existed until you see it for the first time in the light of morning." It was easier not to think of it.

Thirty-five, thirty-six, thirty-seven . . .

A great lumpty thing one never saw before. Not only ecstasy and joy and an occasional feeling of overpowering peace, but also guiding and protecting and watching and hoping, grieving and planning and seeing all one's plans go awry. "I did not agree to be tied to any great, demanding responsibility," she said, surprised at how clearly this came. "I don't want to be tied to it."

"Come now," said a commentator. "You don't know what it is yet. You think it's likely to be lumpty, but it might not be that bad. You haven't seen it. How would you know?"

"I know," said Mavin, scowling to herself. "Never mind how I know, I know."

"She knows," said the wind. "Silly girl," commented the trees. Her inner voices agreed with these comments and were silent.

She tried to estimate how far she might be from the Lake of Faces. Two days perhaps, or three. The Lake was a good way south of Chamferton's aerie, of course, and the road lay north. It was probable a great deal of distance could be saved if she could cut cross country southeast to intercept the canyons north of Pfarb Durim. Shadows lay beneath the trees to the southeast. Everywhere except on the road. Benign or malign. Both looked superficially the same until they moved, quivered, flew aloft in sucking flakes of gray. Better not tempt them. Run on.

Ninety-nine, one hundred, start over.

"You loved him as Fon-beast," her internal commentator suggested, as though continuing a long argument. "When you ran wild in the forest. Why do you disavow him now, at the end of a halter?"

"Because," she hissed. "I am tied to the other end of it! If he is tied, we are both tied. Now, voices, be still. Be done. I will think on it no more, care about it no more, worry it no more. I have leagues to run before I can rest upon these stones, and leagues again tomorrow. I run to save my life and Himaggery's life and Arkhur's life, and there is no guilt in that, so be done and let me alone."

This exorcism, for whatever reason, seemed efficacious. She ran without further interruption to her concentration until darkness stopped her feet. She thought she would have no trouble sleeping then, though the stone was of a hardness which no blanket was adequate to soften. She would still sleep, no matter what, she thought, but that supposition was false. She lay half dozing, starting awake at every sound, realizing at last that she heard a Harpy scream in each random forest noise. When she realized that, she remembered also that she was traveling back toward the Lake of Faces, back toward the Harpy's own purlieus. It would be impossible to avoid them there. Impossible to avoid those eyes, those mouths, those long, snaky necks. She fell at last into shuddering dream, in which she was pursued down an endless road, Harpy screams coming from behind her, and she afraid to turn and see how many and how near they were.

She woke to music, thinking for a time in half dream that the Band had come to chase the Harpies away, or had not gone on, or had come back for her.

"Now we sing the song of Mavin," a small voice sang. Actually, it sounded more like "Deedle, pootle, parumble lalala Mavin," but she knew well enough what it meant. In half dream she knew that voice as from a time long past when she had wandered the shadowmarches with the shadowpeople, hearing their song. Half awake, she identified it.

"Proom?" she called, sitting upright all in one motion. "Is that you?" only to have the breath driven out of her as something landed on her lap. Proom. Plus several other shadowpeople, their delighted faces beaming up into her own from between huge, winglike ears while others of their troop pranced and strutted around her.

"Proom, you haven't grown older at all." She was astonished at this, somehow expecting that he would have turned gray, or wrinkled, or fragile. Instead he was as wiry, sleek and hungry as she remembered him, already burrowing into her small pack to see what food she had to share. "There's nothing there, Proom. I'll have to go hunting. Or you will."

He understood this at once, rounding up half his troop with a few high-pitched *lalalas* and vanishing into the forest. She started to cry out a warning, then stopped. There were no shadows within sight. What had seemed ambiguous the day before was clear enough today. Where the shadowpeople had gone there were no shadows except the benign interplay of sun and shade.

A pinching made her gasp, and she looked down to find two of the shadowperson females with their huge ears pressed tight to her stomach. "I know I rumble," she commented, a little offended. "I'm hungry."

The two leapt to their feet, smiling, caroling, dancing into and out of her reach in a kind of minuet. "Obbla la dandle, tralala, lele, la," over and over, a kind of chant, echoed from the forest, "lele, la." They were back in a moment, one with ear pressed against her belly while the others paraded about miming vast bellies, sketching the dimensions of stomachs in the air. "Lele, la," making a great arc with their hands. "Lele, la."

She did not understand. Even when their miming became more explicit she did not understand. Only when Proom emerged from the trees to caress one of the females, gesturing a big belly and then pointing to the baby she carried, did Mavin understand. "No," she said, laughing. "You're mistaken."

"Lele, la," they insisted, vehemently. "Lala, obbla la dandle."

"Oh, by all the hundred devils," she thought. "Now what idea have they swallowed whole. I am not lele la, couldn't be. I haven't . . ."

"In the lovely valley," sang one of her internal voices, using the tune of a drinking song Mavin remembered from Danderbat Keep. "In the lovely valley, see the beasties run. . . ."

"That's not possible. Himaggery was a Singlehorn. I was a Singlehorn. I mean, he thought he was. I really was. Besides, I was only there a day or two. Or ten. Or . . . I don't know how long I was there. How could I know?"

"Lele, la," sang the shadowpeople, seeing her tears with great satisfaction. In their experience human people cried a lot over everything. It took the place of singing, which, poor things, most of them seemed unable to do. There was one group of humans who sang quite well—all males, back in a cliffy hollow west of Cagihiggy Creek. And there was a house of singers in the city of Leamer. Other than the people in those places, most humans just cried.

One of the females crawled into Mavin's lap and licked the tears off her cheek. "Lele, la," she affirmed. "Deedle, pootle, parumble, lalala Mavin."

She, Mavin, even while being sung of at great length and with considerable enthusiasm; she, Mavin, awaiting breakfast; she, Mavin, still disbelieving, stood up to look about her at the world. Some clue was there she had missed. She had been so focused on the shadows, she had not seen the purple lace of Healer's balm under the trees, the seedpods nodding where yellow bells of startle flower had bloomed twenty or thirty days before. So. It was not a matter of a day or two. The startle flower had carpeted the forest north of Chamferton's tower. Now it was gone to greenseed, the pods swelling already.

"It's not possible." She said this firmly, knowing it was a lie, trying to convince herself.

"It is possible." She said this firmly, too, knowing it was true, trying to convince herself.

"Lele, la," sang the female shadowpeople, welcoming the males back from their foraging in the woods. They came out singing lustily themselves, bearing great fans of fungus, skin bags full of rainhat fruit, and the limp forms of a dozen furry or feathered creatures.

"Celebration," she said to herself in a dull voice of acceptance. "We're having a celebration."

Fires were lit. Mavin was encouraged by pulls and tugs to help prepare food; there was much noise and jollification until she laughed at last. This was evidently the signal they had waited for. The shadowpeople cheered, danced, sang a new song, and came to hug Mavin as though she had been one of their children.

"Well, why not," she wept to herself, half laughing. "Why not. Except that I should not Shift for a time, it is no great burden. And perhaps a child will be company."

"Of course," soothed an internal voice. "Except that you should not Shift for a time." Which was what it had been saying all the while. So she had known it herself. With a Shifter's intimate knowledge of her own structure, how could she not have known it? Known it and refused to admit it.

And that was it, of course. Her protection, her Talent, her experience—all useless for a time. Singlehorn and Arkhur behind her, depending upon her to do a thing which would be easy for a Shifter but perhaps impossible for someone without that ability. Harpies before her, threatening her, quite capable of killing her. If not easy, it would have been at least possible to defeat them so long as she could Shift. And now . . . now!

If Shifting were simply impossible, the matter would be simpler. If she couldn't do it, then she couldn't—there would be no decisions to make, no guilty concerns about choices that should have been made the other way. She would live or die according to what was possible. But the the ability to Shift was still there. If she abstained it was only that an internal voice had told her to abstain—in order to protect what lay within. Old taboos, childhood prohibitions, little brother Mertyn's voice coming back to her out of time, "Girls aren't supposed to, Mavin. They say it messes up their insides. . . ."

Was that true? Who knew for sure? And how did they know? So now, Mavin, believe in the old proscriptions and you will not Shift until this child is born. So now, Mavin, do not Shift and it may be you cannot accomplish what you have set out to do, in which case Himaggery could suffer, even die because of it. Protect the one, lose the other.

"I did not want this lumpty thing all full of hard choices," she cried, tears running down her face. "I did not want it."

"Lele, la," sang the shadowpeople, happy for her.

When the food was cooked, they ate it. The shadowpeople preferred cooked food, though they would eat anything at all, she suspected, including old shoes if nothing else were available. They licked juice from their chins and munched on mushroom squares toasted above the fires, nibbling rainhat berries in between with dollops of stewed fern. When they had done, with every bone chewed twice, they sat across the ashes, stomachs bulging, and looked expectantly at her. This was Mavin Manyshaped of whom a song had been made, and they would not leave her unless they determined that nothing interesting was likely to happen. There were babies present who had never seen her before, this Mavin who had been to

Ganver's Grave, who had saved the people from the pits of Blourbast. So they sat, watching her with glowing eyes, waiting for her to do something of interest.

At last, in a bleak frame of mind which simply set all doubts aside for the time, she stood up, brushed herself off, and waited while they packed up their few bits and pieces; a pot, a knife, a coil of thin rope, the babies clutching tight to their neck fur. Then she went to the side of the road and built a cairn there with a branch run through its top to point a direction. All the shadowpeople understood this. She was leaving a sign for someone who followed. They chattered happily at this opening gambit, then went after her as she ran off the road toward the southeast, shadows or no shadows. She thought it likely the particular shadows she most feared did not come near the shadowpeople. Perhaps the shadowpeople were immune. Perhaps, like the people of the marching Band, they created an aura which shut such shadows out. For whatever reason, she believed herself safe while with them and chose to use that time in covering the shortest route possible.

The hearty breakfast made her legs less weary, the day less gray than before. The members of the troop gathered foods as they ran close about her, the little ones darting ahead to leap out at them from behind trees or dangle at them from vines broken loose from the arching trees. Mavin stopped from time to time to leave sign along their way, though a blind man could have tracked them by the plucked flowers and the dangling vines. A warm wind came out of the south, carrying scents of grass so strong she might have been running beside mowers in a haymeadow. "Diddle, dandle, lally," the people sang, skipping from side to side. One who had not heard their songs translated might think them simple, perhaps childish. Mavin knew better. Childlike, yes. But never simple. Their tonal language concealed multiple meanings in a few sounds; their capacity for song carried histories in each small creature's head. "Diddle, dandle, lally," they sang, and Mavin made up a translation, wishing the translator-beast, Agirul, were present to confirm it. "I sing joy and running in the bright day, glory in the sun, happiness among my people." She would have wagered a large sum that it was something like that. "I sing babies playing hide and seek in the vines."

This was a good song to run by, and it kept her mind away from her destination. Away from Harpies. The shadowpeople were an excellent distraction and she blessed them as she ran, thanking their own gods for them. It was hard to be really afraid among them, for they faced fear with a belligerent, contagious courage.

When they rested at noon, she acted a play for them, showing herself sleeping first, then acting the part of one who came and stole her face, taking it away, placing it upon a high pole. When she had acted it twice, one of the people began to chatter, dancing up and down, gesturing at the trees, climbing one to a point above her head, hanging there as he mimed a face hanging there, touching the eyes, then his eyes, nose, then his nose, the mouth, then his own, showing them what hung upon the tree. At this they all fell into discussion some pointing eastward of the way they ran, others to the south, waving their arms in violent disagreement. When it was obvious they could not agree, Proom spoke sharply, almost unmusically, and a young one climbed the nearest tall tree to sing from the top of it toward the south and east. After a time, they heard a response, a high, faint warble like distant birdsong. Time passed. The people did not seem distressed or hurried. More time passed. Then, when the sun stood well after noon and Mavin was beginning to fidget, the high, faint birdsong came again, and the shadowman above them warbled his response before plunging down among the branches. He gestured the direction and all of them pounded into movement again, this time guided by infrequent calls which seemed to emanate from distant lines of hill.

Somewhere, Mavin told herself, there are shadowpeople who know the Lake of Faces—perhaps even now they are near there. So the call goes out and is relayed across the forests until someone responds, and then that response is relayed back again. Song-guided, we go toward a place we cannot see. So they went until evening fell and the shade of the trees drew about them. Once more the fire, the foraging, the songs, the laughter. Once more lele-la, and choruses of joy. "I am unworthy of the great honor you do me," said Mavin, bowing until they fell over one another in their amusement. "I am deeply touched."

In the night she dreamed once more, starting upright in the darkness with a muffled scream. In dream the Harpies had laid their talons upon her, she had felt their teeth. The dark around her bubbled with small cries of concern, small soothing songs. Poor lele-la, they sang. She is not used to it yet. After a time, the songs became a lullaby and she slept.

When morning came, they could hear the guilding calls more clearly, this time with something of warning in them. Proom pulled at Mavin's leg, asking to be taken up on her shoulders as he had ridden in the past. At first she thought he was weary of the long run, then she realized he wished to gain height in order to see better what lay before them. Two of the shadowmen ran far ahead this day, darting back from time to time. As noon grew near, they came back from their scouting with a rush of whispered words, and all the troop then went forward at a creep, silent through the brush, seeing light before them at the forest's edge. It was not only the edge of the trees, but also the edge of the land where it fell away in steep cliffs down which streams trickled in a constant thin melody.

She had not seen it from this angle before, but when she looked down, screening her face behind a small bush, Mavin knew where she was. The Lake of Faces lay immediately below them. Had she been able to Shift, she could have swarmed down the cliff and finished her business within the hour. Had she been able to Shift—had the place been untenanted.

It was not only occupied but guarded. At the edge of the trees below were high, square tents of crimson stuff, main poles poking through their scalloped roofs like raised spears. From these poles limp pennants flapped, the device upon them raising old memories in Mavin. She had seen that Game symbol before. It had been blazoned on the cloak and breastplate worn by Valdon Duymit long ago in Pfarb Durim. So. The Demesne of the High King in the person of his thalan-son, Valdon.

Aside from these tents and the armsmen lounging outside them, there were other occupants of the place. She shuddered, sank her teeth into her arm and bit down to keep from crying out. They were there, like giant storks, their white breasts flapping as they walked among the faces, their heads thrown back in crowing laughter so that she seemed to look down their throats, their endless, voracious throats. And he whom she had called the High Wizard Chamferton, strolling there without a sorrow in the world. Mavin stopped biting herself with a deep, gulping sigh. She had hoped it would be easy; she had hoped it would be *possible*. Now what?

She rolled away from the rim of the cliff into the mossy cover of the trees, the shadowpeople following her, silent as their name.

Chapter 7

When she had recovered a little, the first thing which came into her head was that she wished to hear what Valdon and the false Chamferton—what had his brother called him? Dourso? —what those two would talk of. The fact they were here together said much: much but not enough. There was Game afoot, Game awing, Game doing something and going somewhere. Shifty Mavin was angered enough by that to ignore all the lumpty responsibilities and hard choices in an instantaneous retreat to a former self. "I need to get where I can hear them," she growled to the shadowpeople, adding to herself—purely as an afterthought—"Without being seen by the Harpies. And without Shifting."

Proom seemed to understand this well enough, even without an Agirul translator present or a lengthy mime session. Perhaps spying out the ground was a routine first step prior to any interesting thing—a bit of sneaking and slying to learn what was going on. At any rate, he fell into discussion with his fellows, much whispered trilling and lalala, hands waving and eyebrows wriggling, ears spread then cocked then drooped, as expressive as faces. Several of them ran off in various directions, returning to carry on further conversation before inviting her in the nicest way to accompany them. She was not reluctant to go, though doubtful they had found any suitable way down those precipitous cliffs, and was thus surprised to find almost a stair of tumbled stone leading down behind one of the falls. The bottom of it was screened behind a huge wet boulder, and this way led to a scrambly warren among the stones and scattered trees at the foot of the cliffs which emerged at last within two strides of Valdon's tent, the whole way well hidden.

Proom had his neck hair up and his ears high, both expressing self-satisfaction, so she bowed to him, then he to her, then both together, trying not to make a sound, at which all the others rolled on the ground with their hands clamped over their mouths. There was nothing funny in the situation but she relished their amusement. They lay beneath the stone together, waiting for dark. Mavin could hear the Harpies screeching away at the far edge of the lake. They were a good distance away and she could relax enough to plan.

Tomorrow the pombi should reach them, the pombi and Singlehorn. She hoped it would be sooner rather than later, the help of the Wizard being much desired. If she had been able to Shift, she told herself, she would have crept into Valdon's tent at once, strangled him, then swumbled up his men at arms. Then . . . then she would have laid some kind of nasty trap for the Harpies. Yes. Something clever, so that she would not have to touch them. After which the Faces could have been taken care of with simple dispatch. As it was . . . well, as it was she would have to think about it.

Just as dark was beginning to fall, there was a clucking Harpy chatter from the shore of the lake, and the false Chamferton came strolling along the water to be greeted by one of Valdon's men. He disappeared into the nearest tent. The Harpies who had followed him scratched among the poles, pausing now and then to caw insults at the silent Faces. Foulitter carried the wand in its case upon its back. Soon they went back the way they had come, disappearing among the white poles in the dusk. Mavin unclenched her teeth and wriggled from behind the stones, barely aware of the shadowpeople who followed, each mimicking her movements as though they reflected her in a mirror. When she reached the back of the tent she lay still, head resting upon her arms as she strained to hear whatever was said inside.

The false Chamferton was speaking. "Two days ago . . . knew something had happened . . . should have at the time . . . "

"You should have done many things at the time!"

Valdon's voice was raised, easy to hear, stirring memories in her of a long ago time. He sounded no less arrogant now than he had done twenty years before.

"Had you the wits the gods gave bunwits, you would have done many things differently. Eight years ago you engaged upon this elaborate scheme concerning your brother, the Wizard Chamferton. Why did you not merely kill him? Dead is dead, and it is unlikely a Necromancer would seek him out among the departed. But no. You must do this painstaking stupidity, this business of drugging him and having him dropped by Harpies. Why?"

"Because it could have been to our advantage, Prince Valdon. I set him where he could observe the shadow and the tower, the tower and the bell. I kept his Face here to answer my questions. So we might have learned much of mystery and wonder. . . ."

"Dourso, you're a dolt! Mystery is for old men teaching in schools because they have no blood left to do otherwise. Wonder is for girls and pawns. But power and Game—that is for men. Save me from puling Invigilators who seek to outplay their betters. . . ."

"You are in my demesne, Prince." The voice was a snarled threat. "Shouldn't you mind your tongue."

"I am in my own demesne wherever I go, Dourso. You ate my bread and took my coin for decades among the least of my servants. Oh, it's true you had some small skill in treachery. Nothing has changed. You have had possession of a tower for a few years. You have learned a few tricks for a time. Do not overestimate the importance of these trifling things."

"I have them at your instigation," Dourso hissed again. "Let us say at your command. It was you bid me come here and rid the land of the High Wizard Chamferton, taking his place in order that Valdon, King Prionde's son, might have an ally to the north.''

"Well, and if I did? I said rid the land, not encumber it further with enchantments and bother. Let be. What is the situation now?''

"It is no different than it was an hour ago, or a day ago. When I drugged my brother—half brother, and on the father side, which makes it no kind of treachery—I had my Harpies drop him in the valley where the Shadow Tower is. None can come near that place without being shadow-eaten, so it seemed safe enough. . . .''

"Seemed," snorted Valdon in a barely audible voice.

"Seemed safe enough,'' repeated Dourso. "I took his Face before he was drugged, but I never questioned it. There was no need to question the Face. I knew where he was. The Harpies swore to it under pain of my displeasure. That same year came the Wizard Himaggery in search of Chamferton, as you had said he would.''

"In pursuit of an old tale I had taken some pains to see he learned of. His eccentricities were well recognized among more normal Gamesmen. It was not difficult.''

"Well, so he came, bringing with him two old dames from Betand. I fed him the stories we had agreed upon, all of which are true enough, and he went off in pursuit of the runners and the tower. I took his Face before he left, also—though he did not know it—and the Face of one of the old dames as well. She was so far gone that the taking killed her, so it is as well he did not know of that either.''

"So Himaggery came and went, and after a time . . . ''

"After a time, not long after he left, his Face began to answer that it was under Bartelmy's Ban. Then I thought to question the Face of my brother, and so spoke the Face of Chamferton also. Thus I knew one fate had taken them both. So, I said to myself, Himaggery and Chamferton have both been shadow-eaten, and my friend and ally, Valdon, will be mightily pleased. As you were, my Prince. As you were. It is not long since you feasted in my tower and told me so.''

"As I might have remained,'' sneered Valdon, "if he had not returned from the shadow gullet after eight years like one vomited up out of the belly of death.''

There was a pause. Mavin could almost see Dourso's shrug. "It was that Mavin, I suppose. You told me years ago she would probably follow Himaggery."

"As I thought she would eventually. Long and long ago she promised to meet him. My brother Boldery told me of it, full of romantic sighs and yearnings—the young fool. And with her gone there would have been only two left upon my vengeance list—her younger brother, Mertyn, and the old fool, Windlow, at the school in Tarnoch."

"Why such enmity? If her brother is much younger than her, he must have been a child at the time. Was it not at the time of the plague in Pfarb Durim? Twenty years ago?"

"Child or not, Mertyn is on the list. Senile fool or not, Windlow is there as well. Woman or not, Mavin shares their fate. What care I what they may have been. They offended me. They did me an injury. If it had not been for Himaggery, and Windlow, and Mavin and her brother, Pfarb Durim would have fallen into the hands of my friend, and thence at least partly into mine. So my friend tells me. And if I had the wealth of Pfarb Durim in my hands, I would not be grodgeling now about the northern lands in search of allies."

There was a long strained silence. After a time, the false Chamferton spoke again. "Well, so, Mavin came as you know, interrupting your own visit to me. And I did the same with her, feigning friendship and helpfulness, giving her bits and pieces of the story, telling her at the last about the runners. And I took her Face as I had the others and sent her off."

"But she did not die, and the others returned from the dead." Prince Valdon spat the words, working himself up into a fury.

"Which is impossible." Dourso was vehement. "No one returns from the tower. It holds fifty generations of questing heroes sleeping the shadow sleep at its gates."

"What is it, this tower?"

Again, Mavin could extrapolate the shrug from the expressive silence. "Something old, from the time before men came to these parts. Something to do with the Eesties. You say you do not care for such things. Well then, it doesn't matter what it is. It is easy enough to stay away from."

"And to get away from, seemingly. At least your brother and Himaggery and Mavin seem to have done so."

"We don't know that. We know only that when Chamferton's Face was questioned yesterday, it did not speak of the Ban as it has spoken in the past. It said other garbled things, speaking of pombis and music. And when Mavin's Face was asked, it, too, spoke of beasts and music. Only Himaggery's face said what it has said for years, that it is under Bartelmy's Ban."

"So it may be they have only exchanged one death for another?" Valdon asked, rather more eagerly than Mavin thought mannerly. "Then they may yet be dead, or as good as."

"I consider it likely. My Harpies consider it probable. They have been full of celebratory laughter all afternoon. I think you have little to concern you, Prince Valdon. Still, we will let tomorrow come and question the Faces once again."

"You will wait until tomorrow comes and question them, yes," Valdon grated in a harsh, imperious voice. "And the day after that, and the day after that, until you have used up whatever lives they might have left in the answering, Dourso. There are more ways to plant a hedge of thrilps than by poking the dirt with your nose, and your maybe this, maybe not approach has not proven satisfactory."

"As my Prince commands," said the other, conveying more ironic acquiescence than obedience. "I had intended to do so in any case."

Well, thought Mavin, squirming back from the tent into the gloom of the rocks. Isn't he a carrier of long grudges. Twenty years of vengeful thought over a few boyish disagreements. "And a lost city," reminded an internal voice. "At least part of one."

She looked over the area. Dark had come with a sliver of moon, enough light to find a Face, perhaps. She thought she could remember where Himaggery's had been, on the far shore of the lake, about halfway between the water and the trees, roughly in line with a great boulder. Where might her own Face be? Somewhere in that forest, hard to see in the dim.

A soft touch on her shoulder turned her. Proom, reaching

out to touch her face, then gesturing away to the poles. Touching her face once more, gesturing away, that questioning gesture. She nodded in great chin wagging agreement and reached up behind her ears as though she untied something there. She moved her hands forward as though she stripped a mask away, then pointed at the mimed mask and said, "Mavin's." She indicated the poles, then gestured to Proom and his fellows as she raised her eyebrows. Could they find her Face? Could they get her Face? There was colloquy among them while she thought further.

Proom had seen Himaggery once, on the side of a hill above Hell's Maw. She reached out to him, went through the dumb show once more, this time naming the mask, "Himaggery's." He cocked his head, thinking. She did it again. "Himaggery's."

Aha. His face lighted up, and he turned to his troop with a lilting quaver of words. "Maggeries, gerries, ees, ees." Proom was becoming Himaggery, miming him, walking with a graceful stride, chin tilted a little in diffidence, face drawn down in a serious expression. For someone only knee high, he looked remarkably like her memory of the tall Wizard. Mavin tittered, smothering the sound, but it had been enough to set them off. In the instant Proom had a parade of Himaggeries, winding their way among the stones. Mavin lay back against a narrow mossy strip between the rocks, weary beyond belief. So. Perhaps they could find her Face, hers and Himaggery's. She would have to look for Chamferton's Face herself. There was no way to describe him to Proom.

The moon sank toward the west. Night birds called from the cliff tops and were echoed from the river bottom. One of the Harpies screamed in the forest, a quavering screech that brought Mavin upright in terror, making her head ache. She pressed her head between her hands, but the pain only worsened, two sharp, horrible stabbings around her ears, as though two knives were inserted there. Just when she thought she could bear it no longer, that she must scream, the pain weakened, became merely sore, throbbing rather than agonizing. Trembling, she dipped a handkerchief in the trickling fall and bathed her face and eyes. Tears spilled onto her cheeks.

She was reluctant to move her head. Pressing the cold, wet cloth around her ears helped a little. She brought it away red with blood.

She was still staring stupidly at the stains when Proom wriggled back through the rocks, holding a thing at arm's distance from him, his lips drawn back in an expression of distaste and fear. He let it fall at her knees, and she recoiled as her own face looked blindly up at her, ragged holes chewed at ear level. Proom had gnawed the strap away which held it to the post. His lips were red, and he bathed them in the stream with much spitting and wiping. When Mavin showed him the wounds at her ears, he recoiled in mixed dismay and horror.

The mask was paper light, like the shed skin of a serpent, fluttering in the light evening air with a kind of quasi life. She held it under the falls, feeling it squirm weakly beneath her hands, suddenly slick as frogskin and as cold. It became a slimy jelly in her hands, then began to dwindle in the cold water, becoming totally transparent before it dissolved and washed away. As it did so, the pain in her head almost disappeared though a quick touch verified that the wounds remained.

Another of the shadowpeople squirmed through the stones bearing a mask. Yes. Himaggery's. Ragged about the upper face as her own had been.

"Gamelords," she cursed to herself. "Did it hurt him as it hurt me?" Knowing even as she said it that it would, that it already had. "He will not understand," she whispered. "Oh, Chamferton, pray you have tight hold upon him!"

Once more she held a mask in the flowing water, feeling the foul sliminess of it soften into jelly before it vanished. The shadowpeople observed this closely as they talked it over among themselves, and Mavin knew that they were resolving to steal others of the Faces now that they knew what to do with them. Not now, though. Now was time for sleep. She had not the energy to do more tonight.

They climbed the stones behind the falls and found a softer bed among the trees. There was no fire tonight, but she lay pillowed and warmed among a score of small bodies, sleeping more soundly than she had upon the Ancient Road.

She was wakened by a startled vacancy around her, a keening cry of panic which dwindled at once into shushed quiet. There was hot breath on her face. The pombi face which stared down into her own had a broken strap in its mouth and an expression of sad determination in its eyes. She struggled out of dream, trying to remember the words of exhortation.

"Come out, Arkhur," she said at last, still struggling to get her eyes fully open. The pombi shape shifted, lifted to its hind feet, solidified into the figure of Chamferton, the strap still in his mouth.

He spat it out. "I lost him. Last night, not far from here. He screamed as though he were wounded, and then dashed away into the trees. The strap broke. I thought of going after him, but it was too dark to trail him and I knew you might need me here."

The first thought she had was that she should feel relieved. She had wanted to be away from the Fon-beast—wanted not to be responsible for him. Now he had gone, and the matter was settled. Except, of course, that it was not. Her eyes filled with tears which spilled to run in messy rivulets down her face, puffy from sleep.

"He ran because he was wounded when one of the shadow-people chewed his mask from the pole. I didn't know that's what would happen, but it did to me as well." She lifted her hair from the sides of her face to show him. "The masks are spiked to the poles, and the little people couldn't pull out the spikes, so they chewed the masks off. We'll have to find him, Chamferton, but it must wait a little. There is Game here against you and Himaggery and me. You were right that we need you here."

She led him to the cliff's edge. They lay there, peering down at the encampment, and Proom's people, puzzled but reassured by the pombi's disappearance, came to lie beside them, waiting for whatever came next. "I don't know how many times they've questioned your Face in the past, Wizard, but they intend to question it every day from now on. More often if they can."

"They can't," he said flatly. "And I doubt if any of the questioning done while I was in the valley will deprive me of life. I feel stronger than when I last saw this place, the strength of anger, perhaps, but nonetheless useful. Now what is to be done?" He began to list.

"First—to get my own Face down from that obscene array. Second—to eliminate one Dourso, and his allies if necessary. Third—to find Singlehorn. Can you think of anything else?"

"Harpies," said Mavin. "I have some cause to think they are dangerous. Pantiquod brought plague to Pfarb Durim, many years ago. Her daughter Foulitter tried to kill me when I was here last. And Pantiquod has threatened me."

"Harpies," he said, as though adding this item to his list. "The first thing I need is my wand. We have no strength to oppose Valdon and his men until I have the wand. Dourso has probably hidden it somewhere in the fortress."

"He has given it into the keeping of Foulitter," she said. "Look beyond that largest pile of stones, against the trees. See where she struts about there. Look on her back when she turns. See! That is the wand. He gave it to her so that she might question certain of the Faces. I caught them at it when I came here first."

"The fool! To set such a thing in a Harpy's hands. They would as soon turn on him as obey him!"

"He has some hold on one of them," Mavin said. "Pantiquod flies free but her daughter's in some kind of durance. He told me he would hold her for some time yet."

"Still a fool. He learned a few words, a few gestures, and fancied himself a Wizard. What he learned was only thaumaturgy, gramarye. Children's things. Well, even children's toys may be dangerous in the hands of a fool, so we must go careful and sly. I need that wand."

Mavin forced herself to move. She wanted nothing to do with the Harpies, but something had to be done. She made a long arm to touch Proom and tug him toward her, pointing at the Harpy, moving back from the cliff edge to mime the storklike walk, the bobbing neck, the head thrown back in cackling laughter. The shadowpeople took this up with great enthusiasm, becoming a flock of birdlike creatures almost instantaneously. She pointed out the wand, then pretended to have one such on her own back, removing and replacing it. Finally, she led them off through the trees. Chamferton had time to grow bored with the view below him before she returned.

"Come on," she said. "We need simple muscle, and all of it we can get. The shadowpeople will lead her into a kind of trap, but they are not big enough to hold her."

The plan had the virtue of simplicity. If the Harpy were typical of her kind, she would pursue any small creature with the temerity to attack her, which Proom or one of his people would do. They would flee away, and the Harpy would follow.

"They'll try to get her when she's alone, not with Panti-quod. It seems the shadowpeople aren't particularly afraid of them one at a time, but they don't want to tangle with two or more. At least that's what I think all their lalala-ing was about. Proom is down there behind the biggest pile of stones. The others are scattered in a long line leading to that rockfall. The tricky part will be at that point. The shadowman will drop down into the rocks. Then another one will show himself halfway up the slope, then another one at the top. If they time it right, it should seem to be one small person the whole time. She can't walk up that slope, but if she's angry enough, she should fly to the top, at which point they'll lead her between these two trees. Then it's up to us, Wizard. Proom left us a knife, and some rope. . . ." She said nothing about her nausea, her revulsion.

"Rope if we can," hissed Chamferton. "I've a use for her alive. But knife if she starts to scream."

Mavin nodded her agreement. From their hiding place they could see between leafy branches to the valley floor. Mavin sharpened her eyes, not really Shifting, merely modifying herself a little, to catch a glimpse of Proom—she thought it was Proom—perched near the edge of the stones. The Harpy was prodding at some bit of nastiness on the ground nearby. Panti-quod had wandered toward the tents. There was a scurrying darkness, a darting motion, and the Harpy leaped into the air like some dancing krylobos, screeching, head whipping about. Proom had bitten her on the leg. Mavin could see the blood. A palpable bite, a properly painful bite but not one which would cripple the creature.

No! Not cripple indeed. She strode toward the stones, head darting forward like the strike of a serpent, jaws clacking shut with a metallic finality. On the cliff top, they gasped; but she had missed. A small furry form broke from cover and fled toward the cliff. The Harpy crowed a challenge and sped after it.

The shadowman fled, darted, dropped into hiding. From another hidey hole not far away, another form popped up and fled farther toward the cliffs. The Harpy strode, hopped, struck with her teeth at the stones, hurting herself in the process so that her anger increased.

"Watch now," hissed Mavin. "They're coming to the cliff."

The quarry disappeared into a cleft between two large stones wet with spray. The Harpy thrust her head into the cleft, withdrew it just in time to see her prey appear briefly halfway up the slope, fleeing upward. It turned to jeer at her, increasing the Harpy's frenzy. She danced, clacked her jaws, spread her wings to rise in a cloud of spray and dust. The quarry on the slope disappeared, only to reappear at the top of the cliff.

"Get your head down," Mavin directed.

They could hear Foulitter's approach, the whip of wings and the jaws chattering in rage. A furry shadow fled between the trees, and the Harpy came after. As she passed between the trunks, Mavin and Chamferton seized her, Mavin holding tight to the wings as she tried to avoid those venomous teeth —without success! The serpent neck struck at her, and the teeth closed on her hand. Fire ran through her, as though she had been touched by acid or true flame, and she cursed as she slammed the striking head away. Chamferton thrust a wad of cloth between the teeth and threw a loop of rope about her feet which he then wound tight around the wings. When he had done, they stepped back breathlessly. The Harpy glared at them with mad yellow eyes, threatening them with every breath.

"She will kill us if she can," said Mavin, gasping, cradling her hand; it felt as though it was burned to the bone.

"She would," agreed Chamferton. "If she could." He took the wand from its case, drawing it from among the coils of rope. "If you watch me now, you must promise never to . . . ."

"Oh, Harpy-shit, Wizard! Oath me no oaths. I've seen

more in your demesne recently than you have. I am no chatter-bird and you owe me your life. So do what you do and don't be ponderous about it.''

"Did she bite you?''

"Yes, damn it, she did.'' Mavin stared at him stupidly. "How did you know?''

"Because you suddenly sounded Harpy bit. We'll take care of it before you leave—must take care of it, or you'll die. Harpy bite is deadly, Mavin. But you're right. I have no business demanding secrecy oaths from one who has saved my life. So go or stay as you like.''

She was curious enough to stay, not that she learned any-thing. She could not concentrate because of the pain in her hand, now moving up her arm. All she saw was waving of the wand, and walking about in strange patterns, and speaking to the world's corners and up and down, and sprinkling dust and sprinkling water, at the end of which time he removed the rag from the Harpy's mouth and turned her loose. "You are my servant,'' he told her in a voice of distaste. "My unworthy ser-vant. Now you will serve me by giving me the name of one of those you have questioned down below—the name of any one.''

The Harpy answered in a toneless voice without pause, "I have questioned Rose-love of Betand.''

"Very well,'' said Chamferton. "When you next hear the words 'Rose-love of Betand,' your servitude is over and you have my leave to die. Do you understand?''

The Harpy nodded, its pale, pendulous breasts heaving. "When I hear the words 'Rose-love of Betand,' I have your leave to die.''

"And you will die then,'' said Chamferton. "Quickly and without pain.''

"And I will die then,'' agreed the Harpy. "Quickly and without pain.''

Chamferton turned away from the empty-faced creature. "The first thing I must do is obtain my own Face.'' Turning to the Harpy, "Go to my Face, Foulitter. Pull the silver spike which holds it to the pole, gently, with your teeth. Bring the Face to me here.''

Without a sound the Harpy walked away to the cliff's edge

and dropped from there on quiet wings to the regiment of pale poles on which the Faces hung. To Mavin, accustomed to the constant cluck and keraw of the Harpies, this quiet evoked more foreboding than sound might have done.

"Is she completely at your command?" Somehow she still doubted this.

"Completely. Though nothing would have put her completely at my command unless she had attempted to injure me first—or had succeeded. There is a rule of Wizardry called the Exception of Innocence. We are not allowed to bind the will of one who has never done us ill or attempted it. It is somewhat inconvenient at times."

"I can imagine it would be," she rasped, glad she had done the High Wizard Chamferton only good. "And what of those who have actually helped you, aided you?"

"No true Wizard would be so unmannerly as to enchant one such," he replied with a smile. It was an ominous smile, for all his appearance of grave, childlike stubbornness. Still, she took it as sufficient encouragement to ask a further question.

"You said something earlier about Dourso having learned only thaumaturgy, gramarye—children's things. Does that mean such things are not the Talent of Wizards?"

"Such things are not. Such things are mere tricks, like the Faces. They are dependent upon a particular place, perhaps a particular time. Did Dourso tell you about the lake? About the nexus here? Blame my stupidity that I bragged to him about it, crowing at my discovery. The crux of the thaumaturgy lies with the lake, with the forces around it. I chose my demesne because of the forces which are here, not the other way around. Away from this place I am no more or less Wizardly than any of my colleagues. Only this place—and that arrogant aerie built halfway to the clouds—gives me the name 'High Wizard'."

"How did you ever learn to . . . to do things. Make the faces. Or bind Harpies. Or whatever?" It was hard to think through the pain in her arm, but she doubted that Chamferton would often be so patient with questions.

"I have speculated about that," he mused. "It is my theory that the forces of the place desire expression. That they, themselves, are my tutors, suggesting to my dream-mind what

I should try or do." He gave her another of those quick, ominous looks. "You have said you are no chatterbird, Mavin, and I rely upon that. I do not want half the world of the True Game camped upon my steps, attempting to learn what I have learned, or—worse—finding out and using it to make more pain and tragedy in this world."

She returned him an enigmatic smile. She had already given him her word; it was not necessary to give it again. Besides, the sound of wings returning drew their eyes to the cliff edge where Foulitter now perched, her teeth broken and bloody around the silver spike and limp Face she carried. Arkhur took it without a word, carrying it to the stream where he pressed it deep into the chill water to let it dissolve, shuddering slightly as he did so.

"I think the shadowpeople intend to remove more of them," Mavin remarked, more to break the silence than for any other reason.

"It won't be necessary," he growled with sudden determination, shuddering again at the feel of the slimy tissue under his fingers. "There will not be any left after today. I have decided that because a thing can be done is not always reason enough to do it." He rose from the stream, face pale, a small muscle at the corner of his eye twitching again and again. "Do you have any idea whose Faces he has taken down there? Dare I hope they are mostly villains? Gamesmen Ghouls, perhaps? What of that one the Harpy named? Rose-love of Betand?"

Mavin shook her head, almost sorry to tell him the truth. "I think it unlikely they are Ghouls and villains, Wizard. Rose-love is one of the old women Himaggery brought from Be-tand, a story-teller. I overheard Dourso say he had taken her Face and killed her doing it. Her sister still lives at the aerie—or did when I was there half a season ago. She, too, is full of old tales. Neither of them were Gameswomen. There were merely . . . people."

"So Dourso has taken Faces from peaceful folk, pawns, perhaps even goodly Gamesmen, Healers and the like?"

"I would not doubt it," she agreed.

"And some of them have lost life, perhaps much life. Some, like old Rose-love, may have lost all life. Whatever is done must seek to set that right. Certainly whatever is done must not put them at further risk. Ah well. I have my wand. I can do what must be done. However, there is a counter spell, and it may be that Dourso has learned it. His understanding is not great, but his sense of power and treachery are unfailing. If he has learned it, then the Faces would be caught between my power and his, possibly injured or destroyed, and their owners would suffer even more.''

"But you have the wand!"

"The counter spell would not require a wand though perhaps he does not know it. Would you risk that?"

Mavin thought of the Faces as she had seen them first in moonlight, unconscious, taken from who knew what persons abroad in the world. "No," she admitted. "I wouldn't risk hurting them any more. Not if there were some other way."

"We will think of some other way. Perhaps we can lure Dourso away from here, back to the aerie, leaving me here alone for a short time. . . . Yes. Back to the aerie with Valdon. Hmmm. Let me think on that."

He strode away toward the cliff top, ignoring the Harpy half crouched there, her nipples almost brushing the ground. The Harpy's face was not unlike those on the poles, blind and unaware, yet full of some enormous potential which was almost palpable. In this case, the potential was for evil, thought Mavin, turning her back on the creature, trying not to vomit at the sight of her. Her arm throbbed and she was full of pain and hunger and annoyance. Waiting on another to take action was foreign to her nature, and she fought down her irritation. She should be away from here, searching for Himaggery.

"Searching for Himaggery," she snarled. "I have done nothing else since first arriving at Pfarb Durim."

A tug at her leg made her look down into Proom's face, wrinkled with concern. Was she sick, unhappy, miserable? Poor Mavin. What would Mavin do now?

"I'm hungry," she announced, rubbing her stomach and miming eating motions. "Let's have breakfast."

He was immediately ready for a feast, slipping away full of song to summon the others. It was not long before they had a fire going, hidden behind piled stones, with chunks of mushroom broiling. Someone had brought in a dozen large, speckled eggs. Surprisingly they were fresh, probably purloined from some farmyard. When the High Wizard finished his solitary walk and sought them out, they were fully engaged in breakfast with little enough left for him.

"I have a plan," he said.

Mavin nodded, her mouth full. She would listen, the nod said, but she didn't feel it necessary to stop chewing.

"You will go to the aerie," he said, ticking this point off on one palm with a bony finger. "Seek the Healer. Tell the ones there you have been Harpy bit, need Healing, and have a message for the High Wizard Chamferton—his demesne is threatened from the north. That should get their attention. Someone there will know where the supposed High Wizard is. Insist that a message be sent immediately. Can you ride horseback?"

The question seemed a meaningless interpolation, and it took her a moment to respond. "After a fashion. Why?"

"There is a farm a little east of here where you can borrow an animal in my name. Ride hard as you can to get to the aerie by early afternoon. They will send a messenger back here—to my loving brother, Dourso—that messenger arriving by evening. If the message is properly portentous, Dourso will leave here at once for the aerie, arriving there about midnight. It may be Valdon will go as well, but in any case Dourso will go. That will be enough for my purposes."

"What am I to do there? Merely wait? Or depart again?"

"Well, you are to find the Healer, as I said. You must not let that Harpy bite go untended. The mouths of the creatures are poisonous as serpents'. It is not precisely venom which they hold, but some other foulness which comes from the filth they eat when they are in Harpy shape.

"So, you find the Healer, in private, and tell her I sent you. Say 'Arkhur' so she will know which Wizard you speak of. After she has healed you, secret yourself somewhere within sight of the aerie. It may be you will want to see the end of this matter."

"How will I know when that is?"

"You'll know," he said in a flat, emotionless voice. "You will know." He pulled her to her feet and pointed the direction to the farm he had mentioned. She wiped one hand upon her trousers, cradling the other in her shirt, and awkwardly tied back her hair. Proom had his head cocked in question, and she nodded to him. Yes. She wanted the shadowpeople to come with her. No further word or action was needed. They were packed and ready to go within moments.

She found the farm without trouble. The farm wife heard her out, then went to the paddock and whistled to a sleek brown horse which came to her hand, nuzzling her and her pockets.

"Prettyfoot," cooed the wife. "Will she carry the nice lady and her pet? Hmmm? High Wizard wants us to help the nice lady. Will Prettyfoot do that? Oh, wuzzums, she will, won't she?"

Mavin stared in astonishment at this, but Proom—the only one of the shadowpeople to have accompanied her into the yard—stood nose to nose with Prettyfoot and seemed to sort the matter out. The farm wife went so far as to try to pet him. Proom growled deep in his throat, and her gesture became a quick pat of Prettyfoot instead.

"She'll go best for you at an easy jog," she said, suddenly all business. "Not fast, but steady. When you're arrived where you're going, turn her loose and she'll find her way back to me. I trust you not to abuse her, woman, you and your pet. The High Wizard has not often asked a favor before, though we owe him much at this farmstead."

Mavin promised, helped with the saddle and bridle, and got herself and Proom astride, Proom bounding up and down behind her, making her dizzy by tugging at her sides. Then they were away, and Mavin merely sat still while Prettyfoot jogged off toward the north, tirelessly, and happily for all Mavin could tell. They stopped briefly only once, to drink from a streamlet they crossed, and it was still early afternoon when she saw the aerie towering above a low hill. If she were to talk of threats from the north, she would have to arrive from the north, so she circled widely to the east before dismounting, tying the reins loosely to the saddle and patting Prettyfoot on her glossy flanks. The little horse shook her head and cantered back the way she had come, seemingly still untired. Mavin memorized the animal's shape. It was one she thought she might have use for in the future.

She left Proom in the trees with a stern injunction to stay where he was. Previous experience had taught her to verify this, and she walked part of the distance to the tower backwards, making sure he was not following her. She had no doubt the rest of his family would be with him by the time she returned. If she were able to return. She was staggering rather badly, and her arm felt like a stone weight.

The fortress was as she had seen it last, brooding upon its high plinth, the sun flashing from the narrow windows, the stairway making a pit of darkness into the stone. She approached it as she had before, hammering upon the heavy door with her good hand, hearing the blammm, blammm, blammm echo up the stony corridors within. It was some time before there were other sounds, pattering, creaking, and then the squeak of a peephole opening like an eyelid in the massive wood.

"I come with an important warning for the High Wizard Chamferton," she intoned in her most officious voice, somewhat handicapped by the fact that the world was whirling around her. "Tell him Mavin is here."

"Babble babble, Wizard not at home, babble, grumph, go away."

"When he learns you have disregarded my warning, he will want to know the name of the person who told me to go away. I have no doubt he will repay you properly." She saw two faces at the peek hole but knew there was only one person there. She held up one finger and saw two. "Healer," she begged silently. "Please be at home."

Scuttle from inside, a whiny voice trailing away into distant silence, then the approach of heavier feet. "What do you want?"

"I bring a warning for the High Wizard. First, however, I must make use of his Healer."

The door creaked reluctantly open. "High Wizard isn't here."

"The High Wizard is somewhere," Mavin snarled. "I have no doubt you know where to find him. Best you do so very quickly. Before giving the message, however, I need to see the Healer. Now!"

Orders were shouted in a surly voice. A search took place.

There was running to and fro and disorderly complaints. "Is she in the orchard? Beggle says look in the melon patch. Get Wazzle to come up here."

Mavin sat herself wearily. The world kept fading and returning. At last they found her. Mavin retreated with her into the privacy of a side room, pulling the door firmly shut behind her.

"Harpy bit?" the Healer questioned. "Nasty. Here, give me your hand."

"Arkhur sent me," whispered Mavin, dizzy, distracted, sure there were ears pressed to the door.

"Ahhh," murmured the Healer, gratified and moist about the eyes. "Is he well?"

"Now he is. Now that his Face is taken down from its pole."

"That is good news. Be still, please. I am finding the infection." She nodded at the door, indicating listeners. Mavin sat back and relaxed. There were a few peaceful moments during which the pain lessened, becoming merely a slight twinge, a memory of pain. The throbbing which had pounded in her ears was gone. She sighed, deeply, as though she had run for long leagues.

Then they had done holding hands. The Healer passed her fingers across the wound, already half healed, then across those shallow scrapes around Mavin's ears. These, too, she Healed, making them tingle briefly as though some tiny, marvelous creature moved about raking up the injured parts and disposing of them.

"Now, what's afoot?" the Healer asked, brushing the tips of her fingers together as though to brush away the ills she had exorcised. "What can I do?"

"A message must be sent to . . . the High Wizard Chamferton telling him his demesne is attacked from the north." This was loudly said.

"Ah. Do we know who attacks?"

"The attacker is unspecified," murmured Mavin. Better let Dourso respond to some unknown threat than discount a threat he might know to be false. Loudly: "Unspecified but imminent. He should return here as soon as possible."

"A messenger sent to him now will reach him by dusk. If he

left there at once, the . . . High Wizard might return here by midnight.''

"Whatever," Mavin yawned. "Now, if you have no further need of me, I will take my leave. Send the message quickly, please. Much may depend upon it.''

The Healer gave her one keen glance, then moved away, opened her door to give firm orders to some, quick instructions to others. As Mavin left the place she saw two riders hastening away south in a cloud of dust. She rubbed her face. The area around her ears itched a little, and she smoothed her hair across it self-consciously. Shifters did not make much use of Healers. It had not been as bad an experience as she had thought.

Proom was where she had left him, Proom and his family and his friends. A much wider circle of friends than heretofore. They seemed to enjoy the afternoon, though most of it was spent watching Mavin sleep and explaining to the newcomers that this was, in fact, the Mavin of which many things were snug. Undoubtedly something of interest would occur very soon, and the newcomers were urged to pay close attention. Mavin heard none of it. She had decided to sleep the afternoon away in order to be up and watching at midnight.

Night fell, and there was a foray for provisions followed by small fires and feasting. Smoke rose among the trees, dwindled to nothing and died. Mavin rose and led the shadow-people forth to find a good view of the aerie. Even as they settled upon their perch, Dourso came clattering up to the fortress with Valdon and Valdon's men making a considerable procession upon the road, two baggage wagons bringing up the rear. A large, grated gate opened at ground level to admit the wagons, the horses and most of the men. Valdon and Dourso climbed to the door Mavin had used, and not long afterward she saw lights in the highest room of the tower.

"May neither of them have time to get their breath back," Mavin intoned, almost enjoying herself. She had found a grassy hollow halfway up the outcropping on which the aerie stood. She could see the road, the aerie, the doorway—even the roof of the melon patch gleaming a glassy silver in the moonlight. "Now Dourso will be looking north to see what comes." She sipped at the wine the Healer had given her, offering some to Proom. He took a tiny taste and handed it back, nose wrinkled in disgust. "Well, beastie," she commented, "to each his own taste. I've never really liked those stewed ferns everyone cooks each spring, though most people consider them delicious. Now. What's that upon the road?"

It was an ashen shadow, a bit of curdled fog, a drift of clotted whey. It moved not with any steady deliberation but in a slow, vacillating surge, like the repeated advance of surf which approaches and withdraws only to approach once more. Though Mavin sharpened her eyes, she could see no detail. It came closer with each passing moment, the shadowpeople staring at it with equal intensity.

"Lala perdum, dum, dum," Proom whisper-sang. "Ala, la perdum."

"I don't know what perdum is." Mavin stroked him. "But I'm sure we're going to find out."

"Perdum." Proom shivered as he climbed into Mavin's lap. She had seen him thus disturbed only once before, many years ago in the labyrinth under Hell's Maw, and she closed her arms protectively around him. "It's all right, Proom. Whatever it is, it isn't coming for us."

The cloud came nearer, still in its clotted, constant surge and retreat. She peered in the dim light, suddenly knowing what it was. "Faces," she cried. "All the Faces. There must be thousands of them. And they have their eyes open!"

Through the milky cloud she could make out Arkhur's form on horseback, with the striding Harpy behind him as he set the pace for the floating Faces in their multitude. Proom whispered from her lap, a hushed, horrified voice. She could see why. The mouths of the Faces were open as well, hungering.

From the high tower the northern windows flashed with light, now, again, again. Whoever watched from there did not see the threat approaching on the southern road. Mavin had time to wonder how the Faces would assault the fortress, or whether they would simply besiege the place. She did not wonder long. The cloud began to break into disparate bits, a hundred Faces there, a dozen here, here a line trailing off up the stony plinth like a dim necklace of fog, there a small cloud gathering at the foot of the great door. There was no frustration of their purpose. The door presented no barrier to their paper thinness. They slipped beneath it easily, as elsewhere they slipped through windows and under casements, between bars and through minute cracks in stone. Within moments all were gone.

Silence.

Silence upon the height, the light still flashing to the north.

Silence within the aerie, the stables, the armories.

And then tumult! Screams, shouts, alarm bells, the shrill *whee*ing of a whistle, the crashing sound of many doors flung open as people tried to flee.

Did flee. Down the steps of the fortress, out of the great gates. Beating with arms and hands as though at a hive of attacking bees while the Faces clustered thickly upon those arms, those hands, around mouths, clamped upon throats. A man ran near the hollow where Mavin sat, screaming a choked command as a Face tried to force its way into his throat. It was Valdon, all his arrogant dignity gone, all his Princely power shed, running like an animal while the Faces sucked at him with pursed, bloody lips, to be struck aside, only to return smiling with manic pleasure as they fastened upon him once more.

Mavin turned away, unsure whether she was fascinated or sick. On the flat below ran a half-dozen others, Dourso among them, so thickly layered with Faces it was only their clothes which identified them. Some of Valdon's men. Some of Dourso's. Yet even as these ran and choked and died beneath the Faces, others walked untouched. The Healer, quiet in her white robes, came down the steps to stretch her hand toward Arkhur, to cling first to his hand and then to his body as though she had not thought ever to see him again. So, thought Mavin. So that is what that is all about. Something in her ached, moved by that close embrace.

Valdon had fallen. One by one the Faces peeled away, eyes closed once more, mouths shut. Misty on the air they hung, fading, becoming a jelly, a transparency, a mere disturbance of sight and then nothing. Unable to stop herself, she went to the place the body lay, prodded it with her foot. It swayed like a bundle of dried leaves, juiceless, lifeless.

"There are two ways to dispose of the Faces," said Chamferton's voice from behind her. "To dissolve them in running water, or to let them regain whatever life was taken from them. Come in and we will see what has been done." He turned toward the fortress and Mavin followed, the shadow-people staying close by her feet. The Harpy stalked behind them without a sound, but still Mavin shuddered to come near her. They passed up the great stairs, through the door, down a long, echoing corridor to stop before a narrow door behind an iron grate. On this door, Chamferton knocked slowly.

"Who's there," quavered an old voice. "Who is it there?"

"Who is it there?" Chamferton responded.

"I?" asked the weak old voice, wonderingly. "I? Why I am Rose-love of Betand. . . ."

Behind them the Harpy slumped dead to the floor.

"What's in there?" asked Mavin, not really wanting to know.

"The tombs of my demesne," said Chamferton. "Healer? Will you have her taken out of there and up to her sister's room? Chances are she will not live out a year, but such time as it is, it is hers. Recovered from Dourso's blood and bone.

"None of the Faces has lost life. The Faces themselves are gone. Valdon and Dourso are dead. Foulitter is dead. Only Pantiquod was left behind at the lake, and she fled before I could bind her. I believe she has gone to the south, Mavin. It is unlikely she will return to the north."

Mavin heard him without hearing him. She wanted to believe what he said.

They found the room Mavin remembered from her prior visit, and there were summoned the people remaining in the place, many of them suffering from wounds or minor enchantments. Some were Healed, some disenchanted, wine was brought, and while the shadowpeople roamed about the room, poking into everything—surprisingly free of the place, inasmuch as Mavin had never seen them enter human habitation before—Chamferton turned the talk to Singlehorn.

"It will be a search of many days, I fear," he said in a tired voice, obviously not relishing further travel. She saw the way his eyes searched the shelves, the corners, knowing that he found it defiled and would not be content until he could replace it as it had been. "A search of many days."

"No," Mavin said. "It shouldn't take that long. I could

find him almost at once if I could only tell the shadowpeople what he looks like. I can convey only so much in mime. Trying to describe the beast is beyond me."

The Healer had followed all this with interest, though never moving from Chamferton's side. For his part, he seemed to be conscious of her presence as he might be conscious of his own feet or ears, giving her no more of his attention than he paid those useful parts. She laid her hand on his arm.

"Old Inker is still here, Arkhur. Couldn't he do a picture for the little people?"

So in the end it was very simple. Mavin described while an old, sleepy man drew a picture, this way and that until he had it right; then he put it in her hand and staggered back to his bed.

"I will come with you," offered Chamferton without enthusiasm, examining a pile of books.

"No," she said, knowing he would be little help. If he came with her, his mind would be here. "The shadowpeople will find him. I have only to follow. But I would like to know one thing, High Wizard, before I go."

"If I know whatever it is."

"What is the tower? The one where you were dropped? What are the shadows? Why did Himaggery want to find it, and how did he get in without being eaten?"

He stared at her for such a time that she felt he had stopped seeing her, but she stood under that gaze neither patiently or impatiently, merely waiting. Proom and his people were lying quietly about, silent for once, perhaps composing a song to memorialize the destruction of the Lake of Faces.

When he replied it was not in the ponderous, Wizardly voice she had begun to associate with him. It was rather doubtful, tentative.

"Do not talk of it, Mavin. When Himaggery is brought back to himself, discourage him from having interest in it. Though I have read much, studied much, I understand very little. I will say only this . . .

"Before men came to this world—or to this part of the world, I know not which—there were others here. There was a balance here. You may say it was a balance between shadow and light, though I do not think what I speak of can be described in such simple terms. One might as well say power and weakness, love and hate. Of whatever kind, it was a balance.

"There was a symbol of that balance. More than a symbol; a key, a talisman, an eidolon. A tower. In the tower a bell which cannot ring alone. Ring the bell of light, and the shadow bell will sound. Ring the shadow bell and the daylight bell will resonate. So was the balance kept. Until we came. Then . . . then something happened. Something withdrew from this world or came into it. The tower disappeared or was hidden. The bell was muffled. . . .

"An imbalance occurred. Does the real tower still exist? Is the bell only muffled? Or destroyed? Does something now ring the shadow bell, something beyond our understanding?

"Mavin, do not speak of this. In time the balance must be restored or the world will fail. But I think the time is not now, not yet. Any who attempt it now are doomed to death, to be shadow-eaten. So—when you have brought Himaggery to his own once more, do not let him seek the tower."

Mavin heard him out, not understanding precisely what he attempted to say—and knowing that he understood it no better than she—yet assured by her own sight and hearing that he spoke simple truth as it could be perceived by such as they. She, too, had seen the shadows. She, too, had heard the sound of their presence. It was not the time.

"I will remember what you say, Arkhur," she promised him. Then she took leave of the Healer, accepting many useful gifts, and went out into the dawn.

Chapter 8

At Chamferton's invitation—though it was actually the Healer who thought of it—Mavin took several horses from the stable beneath the rock. None was the equal of Prettyfoot, but any at all would be easier than walking. She rode one and led three, the three ridden—or better, she thought, say "inhabited"—by Proom and his people. They did not so much ride as swarm over, up and down legs, around and across backs. The horses, at first much astonished and inclined to resentment, were petted into submission. Or perhaps talked into submission. Mavin had a sneaky belief supported by considerable evidence that Proom spoke horse as well as fustigar, owl, flitchhawk, and a hundred other languages.

She showed Proom the picture of Singlehorn only after they had found the place from which the Fon-beast had bolted, a place in the woods still some distance northwest of the Lake of Faces (former Lake of Faces, Mavin said to herself, trying to think of a good name for it now). He looked at it with obvious amusement, then passed it around to the accompaniment of much discursive lalala, snatching it back when one infant attempted to eat it.

The search was immediately in motion, with a dozen shadowpeople up as many trees, all twittering into the spring noonday. They descended after a time to swarm over their steeds once more, pointing away to the west and urging Mavin to come along. Calls kept coming throughout the afternoon, always from the west, as they proceeded into the evening until the forest aisles glowed before them in long processionals of sun and shade, the sky pink and amber, flecked with scaly pennants of purple cloud. None of them had slept for a full day and night. Though the guiding song had not yet fallen silent there was general agreement—not least among the horses—that it was suppertime.

They built a small fire and ate well, for the Healer had sent packed saddlebags with them, bags full of roast meat and cheese, fresh baked bread and fruit from Chamferton's glass-houses. Then they curled to sleep—except that they did not sleep. The shadowpeople were restless, getting up again and again to move around the mossy place they had camped upon, full of aimless dialogue and fractious small quarrels. Finally, just as Mavin had begun to drift away, one of them cried a sharp, low tone of warning which brought all of them up to throw dirt upon the coals of the fires.

"Sssss," came Proom's hiss, and a moment later tiny fingers pressed upon her lips.

It took time to accustom her eyes to the dark, though she widened them as much as she could to peer upward in the direction all the little faces were turned, ears spread wide, cocked to catch the least sound.

Then she heard it. The high, shrill screech of a lone Harpy. A hunting cry.

"Pantiquod," she whispered, questioning their fright.

"Sssss," from Proom. A shadowperson was pouring the last of Mavin's wine on the fire while others peed upon it intently, dousing every spark and drowning the smoke.

"Why this fear?" she asked herself silently. "They played tag with Foulitter upon the hill near the lake. They led her into a trap without a moment's hesitation, yet now they are as fearful as I have ever seen them."

The horses began an uneasy whickering, and a dozen of the little people gathered around them, talking to them, urging some course of action upon them and reinforcing it with much repetition. Mavin did not understand their intention until the

horses trotted away into the darkness, returning as they had
come.

"No!" she objected. "I need . . . "

"*Ssss*," demanded Proom, his hands tightening on her face.
Then she saw them. A line of black wings crossing the
moon, beat on beat, as though they breathed in unison, moving from the northeast. From that purposeful line fell a single
hunting call, as though only a lone Harpy hunted there upon
the light wind. Beat on beat the wings carried them overhead,
and as they passed directly overhead Mavin heard a low,
ominous gabble as from a yard of monstrous geese.

They waited in silence, not moving, scarcely breathing.
After a long time, Mavin tried again. "Pantiquod?"

Proom showed his teeth in a snarl. "Perdum, lala, thossle
labala perdum."

"Perdum," she agreed. "Danger." The little ones took this
word and tried it out, "ger, ger, ger," decided they did not
like it. "Perdum," they said, being sure all of them were in ac-
cord. Mavin thought not for the first time that she must learn
Proom's language. Perhaps—perhaps there would be a time
of peace while she waited for her child to be born. Perhaps
then. She considered this possibility with surprising pleasure.
It was ridiculous not to be able to talk together.

Be that as it may, she could appreciate the danger. One
Harpy could be teased, baffled, led on a chase. Perhaps two or
three could be tricked or avoided. But more than that? All
with poisonous teeth and clutching talons? No doubt Pantiquod had learned of Foulitter's death and was out for
vengeance. "Fowl, bird-brained vengeance," she punned to
herself, trying to make it less terrible. Proom had sent the
horses away because they were large enough to be seen from
the skies. So long as those marauders ranged the air, travel
would have to be silent, sly, hidden beneath the boughs. She
hoped that Singlehorn was not far from them and had not
chosen to wander down into the plains or river valleys where
there would be no cover.

At last, having worried about all this for sufficient time, she
slept.

Proom shook her awake at first light, and they made a
quick, cold breakfast as they walked. The twittered directions

came less frequently today, and more briefly. Obviously other shadowpeople went in fear of the Harpies as well. Rather than travel today in a compact group, they went well scattered among the trees, avoiding the occasional clearings and open valleys. When it was necessary to cross such places, they searched the air first, peering from the edges of the trees, then dashed across, a few at a time. Mavin judged that the Harpies were too heavy to perch at the tops of trees—and the thought made her remember the broken vine outside her window at Chamferton's castle—but they could find suitable rest on any rock outcropping or cliff. Proom, well aware of this, kept them far from such places, and they did not see the hunters during the daylight hours.

Nor did they see Singlehorn. That night as they ate another cold meal without the comfort of fire, Mavin remembered that forlorn, bugling call the Fon-beast had sent after the Band as it marched away west. If Singlehorn were following the Band, then he might be moving ahead of them at their own speed. If that were the case, they might not catch up with him until he came to the sea, a discouraging thought. Though the shadows had little interest in him in his present shape, she wondered if the Harpies did.

At midnight she woke to the sound of that lone, hunting cry. There was an overcast, and she could not tell if there were more than one. Around her, the shadowpeople moved restlessly in their sleep.

So they went on. On the third night nothing disturbed them. Proom began to be more his usual self, full of prancing and jokes. The fourth and fifth night passed with no alarms. Mavin had convinced herself that the Harpy flight coming so close to her own path was mere coincidence. As Chamferton had said, Pantiquod had likely gone south to Bannerwell by now. Or somewhere else where her habits and appetites could be better satisfied.

They began to travel on the road which they had paralleled for many leagues. Now they came out upon it, staying close to the edge, still with some nervous scanning of the skies. They could move faster on this smooth surface, and by the time the sixth night fell, Mavin smelled the distant sea.

And on the following morning, a friendly family of shadow-

people drove Singlehorn into their camp, head hanging, coat
dusty and dry, tongue swollen in a bleeding mouth. The
broken strap of the halter still hung from his head, making
small, dragging serpents' trails in the dust. Mavin lifted Fon-
beast's head and looked into dull, lifeless eyes. She growled in
her throat, hating herself for having wanted him gone. There
were swollen sores around his ears, and remembering her own
pain and the gentleness of the Healer, Mavin cursed her impa-
tience with him. And with herself, she amended. It was not
the Fon-beast himself, but her feelings about him that disturbed her. "I will forget all that," she resolved in a fury of
contrition. "I will forget all that and concentrate on taking
care of him until we get to Windlow's."

They gave him water. She squeezed rainhat fruits into his
mouth. Obviously he had not eaten well in the days he had
been gone, or rather he had tried to graze on common grasses.
Though he thought himself a grazing beast, the grasses had
not been fooled. They had cut his mouth and tongue until
both were swollen and infected. Mavin made a rich broth of
some of the meat they had carried and dropped this into his
mouth from a spoon while infant shadowpeople rubbed his
dusty hide with bundles of aromatic leaves.

She had not noticed that Proom had left until he returned
with a group of the older shadowpeople carrying bags full of
herbs and growths, most of which she had never seen before.
These were compounded by the tribe in accordance with some
recipe well known to them all. It resulted in a thick, green goo
which Proom directed be plastered around Singlehorn's
mouth and upon the open sores. Some of it trickled into the
Fon-beast's mouth as well, and Mavin was restrained from
wiping it away. Finally, when everything had been done for
him that anyone could think of, she covered him with her
cloak and lay down beside him. After a time the smell of the
herbs and the warmth of the day made them all drowsy—they
had been much awake during the past nights—and they slept
once more.

When they awoke in the late afternoon, the Singlehorn was
on his feet, pawing at the ground with one golden hoof, nodding and nodding as though in time to music. Dried shreds of
the green goo clung around his mouth and ears. Beneath this

papery crust the flesh was pink and healthy-looking, the swelling reduced; and while his eyes were still tired, he did not look so hopeless. There was a pool a little distance away, and while the shadowpeople yawned and stirred, readying for travel, Mavin led him there. She let him out to the length of the new rope she had tied to his halter but did not release him. "No more running away," she said firmly. "Whatever I may feel about this whole business, Fon-beast, however impatient it makes me, we are bound together until we reach safety." And to herself, she said, "And when we reach Windlow's—then we'll see if there is a true tie between us."

Singlehorn, rolling in the shallow water, tossing his head and drinking deep draughts of cool liquid, did not seem to care. She let him roll, unaware of the sun falling in the west, enjoying the peace of the moment. When she returned to the road, the shadowpeople were gone.

"Hello?" she cried. "Proom?"

Only silence. Perhaps a far-off twitter.

"Goodbye?" she called.

No answer.

Well. They had observed and assisted while Mavin had done several interesting things. They had introduced their children to this person. They had, perhaps, made a new song or two—the Lake of Faces was surely good for at least a brief memorial—but now the shadowpeople had business of their own. Mavin had found the creature she sought, and now they might be about their own affairs. She sought the edges of the road for any sign, any trail, but saw nothing.

Nothing . . .

Except a grayness lying quiet beneath a tree. And another superimposed in fluttering flakes upon a copse, wavering the light which passed through it so it seemed to shift and boil.

Her soul fell silent. Shadows from the tower come to haunt her once more. Not upon the road, which still prevented her presence, but nearby. Perhaps the shadowpeople had been shadow-bane, but without them the bane prevailed no longer.

There was nothing for it except to get on to the south. They must come to Tarnoch at last, or so far from the tower that the shadows would give up. Though what they would give up, or how they were here, she could hardly imagine. Was it she who drew them, or Singlehorn? Were they set to follow any who left the Dervish's valley? And if so, until when? Until what happened? Perhaps this was only conjecture. Perhaps they had not followed at all but were everywhere, always, ubiquitous as midges.

To which an internal voice said, Nonsense. You have not seen them in your former travels because they were not in this part of the world before. Now they are, because they have followed you here from the Dervish's valley. But follow you where they will, they did not harm you when you were with the shadowpeople, and they do not harm you if you stay upon the road.

As she walked away, leading Singlehorn, it was to the steady double beat of those words; the road, the road, the road. *"On the road, the old road, a tower made of stone. In the tower hangs a bell which cannot ring alone. One, two, three, four, five . . ."* When she reached one thousand she began again. *"Shadow bell rang in the dark, daylight bell the dawn. In the tower hung the bells, now the tower's gone."*

Why a stone tower? Was it important? She hummed the words, thinking them in her head, then saw all at once how thickly the shadows lay, how closely to the road, how they piled and boiled as she sang.

Gamelords! Was that verse of the weird runners a summoning chant? It could be!

Sing something else. Anything. A jumprope chant. *"Dodir of the Seven Hands, a mighty man was he; greatest Tragamor to live beside the Glistening Sea. Dodir raised a mountain up, broke a mountain down. See the house where Dodir lives, right here in our town. One house, two house, three house, four house . . ."*

The shadows were not interested in this. They dwindled, becoming mere gray opacities, without motion beneath the softly blowing trees.

"Dodir of the Seven Hands, a mighty man to know, every tree in shadowmarch, he laid out in a row. One tree, two tree, three tree, four tree . . ."

It was true. The shadows were fewer. "Well, Mavin," she said, "Chamferton told you not to think of it, so best you not think of it. Sing yourself something old and bawdy from

Danderbat Keep or old and singsongy from childhood, and keep moving upon the southern way." She soothed herself with this, and had almost reached a comfortable frame of mind when she heard the scream, high and behind her. She spun, searching the air, seeing clearly the dark blot of Harpy wings circling upon a cloud.

Pantiquod had found her at last.

Oh, damn, and devils, and pombi-piss. And damn you, Chamferton, that you let her get away.

And damn you, Himaggery. Damn you, Fon-beast. I should raise you out of that shape and let you fight for yourself. Why must I do everything for you?

The Harpy circled lazily and turned away north. Mavin knew she would return. That had done it! There was no way she could face even one Harpy without Shifting. Being Harpy bit taught that. Even a scratch could be deadly. There being no help for it, she went on walking, singing over in her head every child's song she remembered, every chanty learned in the sea villages, even the songs of the root-walkers she had learned in the deep chasm of the western lands across the sea, and these led her to thoughts of Beedie which led in turn to nostalgic longings to be wandering free again. She had not truly wandered free for five years, not since bringing Handbright's babies back to her kin, and the longing to break away from the rigid edges of the road became almost hysteria by nightfall.

Off the road, beneath the trees, her mind sang, *shadows piled up to your knees. Safe from shadows on the road, and you'll feel the Harpy's goad.* She had not seen Pantiquod again, but she knew the Harpy would return in the dark, or on the day which followed, and she would not return alone.

"Now, Mavin," she harangued herself angrily, "this hysteria does not become you. Were you nothing but Shifter all these years? Were you a Talent only, with no mind or soul to call upon except in a twist of shape? Your Shiftiness is still there, may still be used if we need it. It is not lost to us, but by all the hundred devils, at least try to figure out if we're Shifty enough without it. So, stop this silliness, this girlish fretting and whining and use your eyes, woman. Think. Do."

The self-castigation was only partly effective. She tried to imagine it having been administered by someone else—Windlow, perhaps. That lent more authority, and she forced herself to plan. There were narrow alternatives. If she stayed upon the road to be protected from shadows, she would be exposed to the air. *However!* "We came a long way from the Dervish's valley to this road, and though the shadows swarmed all about us, we were not hurt. Use your head, woman!"

She set herself to watch the shadows instead of ignoring them. How did they lie? How did they move? She watched them for many long leagues, and it seemed to her they moved only in random ways, piling here and there, singly here and there, floating like fragments of gray glass between copses and hills. She tried to foretell where floating flakes would fall. Beneath that tree or upon that clump? Upon the other shadow, or beside it? Where that flock of birds sought seeds among the hedgerows, or beyond them? After a time, she thought she was beginning to be able to predict where the shadow would fall. There was a strange, hazy pattern, if not to their movement, at least to their disposition upon the earth.

If there were any sizeable living thing—any bird or small beast, the shadow would not descend upon that place but in a place near adjacent. The larger the animal or bird, the more thickly the shadows would pile around it, but never upon it and never completely surrounding it. There was always a way out, a trail of light leading through the dark.

She remembered the bird upon the hill. The shadow had not fallen upon it. The shadow had lain there, waiting—waiting for the bird to intrude upon the shadow. And then. . . .

Himaggery had intruded upon the shadow. So said the Dervish.

So had the drugged Chamferton, presumably, though in such a condition that the shadows had not recognized him as a living thing. She saw that the shadows did not seem to bother very small forms of life—beetles and worms went their way beneath the shadow undisturbed.

But larger creatures near which the shadows fell almost always chose the unshadowed way as they hopped about, even when that way was very hard to see—as when the sun was hidden behind clouds, or when the haze of dusk made all things gray and shadowlike.

So. So. One could walk, if one were careful, among the

shadows. One could walk, if one were alert, safely away from the road. She stopped to get food from her pack, to feed Singlehorn, all the time keeping her eyes fixed upon patches of gray in a little meadow to the west of the road. There were gobble-mole ditches druggled through the meadow, dirt thrown up on either side in little dikes, a shower of earth flying up from time to time to mark the location of the mole as it druggled for beetles and worms and blind snakes. The tunnel wound its way among the shadows as though the mole had a map in his snout which told him where they lay.

Could the shadows be sensed in some other way than sight? Perhaps even in the dark? Did they exist in the dark? If one were unaware of the shadows, would one find a safe way among them, without even knowing it? Useless consideration, of course. She did know about them, all too well. But did Harpies—ah, yes, she thought—did Harpies know about the shadows?

Dusk came at last, but well before that she chose the place they would spend the night; a half cave beneath a stone which bulged up from moss and shrub into a curled snout. Shadows lay about it, true, but not in it, and a tiny pool of rainwater had collected at the foot of the stone. They would be comfortable enough, well fed enough, with water to drink and to wash away the dust of the road. They would be unseen from above also, and could lie quiet against the stone, invisible beneath the mixed browns and grays of Mavin's cloak.

Deep in the night she awoke to the first Harpy's cry. Now the variety of cries was unmistakable; the Harpies had returned in force. Why they flew at night she could not tell, unless they relied upon some other sense than sight to find their quarry. Perhaps they, like the huge ogre-owl of the southern ice, cried out to frighten and then struck at the sound of things which fled. Perhaps they did it only to terrify.

"It won't work on me, Pantiquod," she said between gritted teeth. "Go eat a Ghoul or two and die of indigestion." Ignoring the fact that her nails had bitten bloody holes into her palms, she forced herself to sleep. When next she opened her eyes it was day.

Dull day, overcast day, day in which nothing moved and no shadow could be seen against the general murk. She stood at the mouth of the cave, refusing to feel hopeless about the matter but tired beyond belief, wondering what path they might take back to the road. "No panic," she grated. "No hysterics. Quiet. Sensible. You can camp here for days if need be. . . ."

She drew the Singlehorn close beside her, feeding him from her hand. "Fon-beast, sit here by me and keep me warm. We must take our time this morning. I have trapped us by being clever. We must spy out a path."

Which they did, little by little, over the course of an hour, spying where moles moved in the grass, where birds hopped about, where a bunwit mother ran a set of quick diagonals, her two furry kits close behind. They stepped onto the road at last, Mavin with a feeling of relief, the Singlehorn placidly walking behind her. Twice during the afternoon Mavin thought she heard Harpies screaming, but the sound came from above the overcast, remote and terrible, making the Singlehorn flinch and shy against the halter as though he connected that cry with pain.

Toward evening the sky began to clear; and by dusk it held only a few scattered traces of cloud, tatters of wet mist upon the deeper blue. They came to the top of a rise which overlooked a league or more of road, endless undulations of feathery forest, and to the west the encroaching blue of the sea. Mavin began to put landmarks together in her mental map of the area. Schlaizy Noithn lay to the east. Below them the coast began its great eastward curve, and several days to the south they would come to Hawsport, lying at the mouth of the River Haws, full of little boats and the easy bounty of the ocean. Her heart began to lift as she thought of protective roofs and solid inns, sure that the shadows could not gather thickly where there were so many men.

Her elation lasted only for a few golden moments, long enough to make one smothered cry of joy and draw the Fon-beast close to surprise him with a kiss. Then the cry came from the sky behind her, triumphant and terrifying. The Harpies once more.

Harpies. Many more than one. They would not give her time to reach Hawsport and safety. They had played with her long enough, followed her long enough, and now that she was almost within sight of safety they were readying for the kill.

The kill.

Which she might defeat, even now, by Shifting into something huge and inexorable. They were still circling, still flying to get above her. There were a few moments yet. There was time, still, to gain enough bulk for that. Tie the Fon-beast somewhere hidden. Retrieve him later. Build oneself into a wall of flesh which could gather in one Harpy, or a dozen, or a hundred if need be.

An easy, accustomed thing to do.

And then there might be no Himaggery's child and her own.

She considered this for some time. It was by far the easiest solution. Behind her, Singlehorn tapped the stones with his hooves, a jittery dance from one side of the road to the other. Mavin went on thinking, adding to a plan half formed the night before.

"Himaggery," she said at last. "This is as much your doing as mine, and you must share the risk. Come out, Himaggery." She remembered the Dervish's words: *Make him hear you*, and her voice was high-pitched in fear that she would not be able to, in haste and danger.

But the Singlehorn reared to his hind legs, faded, took the form of the man she remembered, the face she had seen a thousand times in reveries, had imagined night and morning over twenty years. His face was full of confusion and doubt. Beyond him on the hillside the air was suddenly alive with shadows, boiling in a frenzy, collecting more thickly with every moment—as she had hoped.

"Go back, Himaggery," she commanded in a stentorian voice allowing only obedience. "Go back!" The man dropped to all fours to become the Fon-beast once more. It stood with its head dragging, discomfitted at this abrupt transformation. The shadows, seeming confused, piled in drifts at the side of the road. The Dervish had been right. The shadows had been seeking Himaggery, and now they were fully alerted to his presence. Her hazardous play depended totally upon what these alert and ravenous shadows would do now with any creature which intruded upon them.

The Harpy cries came once more, nearer. Whirling around, she saw them descending from the north, close enough that she could recognize Pantiquod in the fore. The next step, she reminded herself. Quickly. Do not look at them, do not become fascinated by them. Do not think of them at all, only of what you must do next.

She spun to search the area near the road. There had to be an appropriate battleground near the road, a patch now occupied by some living thing which the shadows had left clear. It had to be close! And it must have a clear trail of light back to the road. She searched frantically, hearing the sound of wings in the height, the cawing laughter of the Harpies as they circled, savoring their intended slaughter.

There it was! A gameboard of light and shadow to the left of the road. A bunwit's burrow in the light, the shadow piled deeply about it, alternate bits of shadow and light leading to it, jump, jump, jump. She pulled the Fon-beast close behind her—he unresisting but unhelpful, subdued, his usual grace gone, almost stumbling after her—hauling him by main strength to keep him away from the shadowed squares, only remembering when she straddled the burrow that she could have tethered him at the road. Well and well. No, the Harpies might have attacked him there. Here at least they stood together upon this tiny patch of sunlight surrounded by piled shadows on every side.

She pushed him to the ground and stood astride him, bellowing a fishwife's scream at the falling fury of wings. He lay dumbly, nose to the ground. "Ho, Pantiquod! Filthy chicken! Ugly bird! Die now as your foul daughter did, and her kin, and her allies. Come feel my claws. . . ."

She had Shifted herself some claws and fangs, needing them badly and considering it no major thing. It was only fingers and teeth, nothing close to the center of her. If so little a thing could destroy the baby within—well, then so be it. Without this much, there would be no chance at all. She danced over the recumbent Singlehorn, screaming abuse at the skies, trying to make the women-creatures furious, frantic, mad with anger, so they would fall to encircle her, come to the ground to use their teeth and talons. They must not drop directly upon her if she could prevent it. She made a long arm to snatch up a heavy branch from the ground, whirling it above her head.

She had succeeded in infuriating them. Their screams were

shattering. They slavered and shat, the nastiness falling around her in a stinking rain. Their breasts hung down in great, dangling udders, swaying as they flew. Beneath Mavin's knees the Fon-beast trembled at the sound of them, even dazed as he was, drawing his legs tight against his body, as though to get out of her way. Mavin whirled the branch above her and taunted them. "Filthy bird. Stinking fowl. Drag-breasted beast!"

Directly above her, Pantiquod folded her wings and dropped like a flitchhawk. Remembering that other flitch-hawk which had dropped upon her at the Lake of Faces, Mavin whirled the branch in a whistling blur of motion.

The whirling branch stopped Pantiquod in her stoop, wings scooped back to break her fall. Around her the other Harpies touched ground, started to strike with talons and teeth only to stop, half crouched, mouths open, panting, panting. Almost all of them had landed in the shadow. Those few which had not beat their wings and leaped on storklike legs to come at Mavin, stepping across their sisters as they did so. Then they too squatted to pant, tongues hanging from wide-opened mouths before they turned their heads to bite at themselves. Then all but the one were so occupied.

She, Pantiquod, was still in the air, still fluttering and screeching threats at Mavin, eyes so closely fixed upon her prey she had no sight to spare for her sisters.

"Filthy chicken," Mavin grated again from a dry throat. "Cowardly hen. When I have finished with you, I will seek out your other children and put an end to them. . . ." This broke the bonds of caution which had held the Harpy high, and she plummeted downward again like a falling stone.

"Strike well, girl," Mavin instructed herself, holding the branch as she had done as a child playing at wand-ball. The stink of the birds was in her nostrils. Her skin trembled with revulsion, and her body threatened to flee with every moment. She gritted her teeth and ignored it. "Strike well. . . ."

As it was, she waited almost too long, striking hard when the foul mouth was only an armspan from her face, swinging the branch with all her strength, unwinding herself like a great, coiled spring.

The branch caught the Harpy full upon her chest. Mavin

heard the bones break, saw the body fall away, half into the shadow. Only half. On the clear ground the head and feet. In the shadow the body and wings. Slowly, inexorably, while the mouth went on screeching and the talons grasped at nothing, the wings drew back into the shadow, back until they were covered.

Mavin looked at her feet. She herself stood within the width of one finger from the shadow. Gulping deeply she drew herself away, drew the Fon-beast away, carefully, and slow step by slow step found a safe path back to the road.

Once there she looked behind her, only once. The shadows were lifting lazily, as though well fed. Behind them on the grass the Harpies flopped, as headless chickens flop for a time, not knowing yet they are dead. Pantiquod was eating herself, and Mavin turned from that sight. Something within her wanted to call out, "Remember the plague in Pfarb Durim, Pantiquod? This is your payment for bringing that plague, Harpy!" She kept silent. She was sure that no creature within the shadow could hear any outside voice. She prayed she would never hear the voice that Pantiquod must be hearing; the voice of the shadow itself.

For a long time she lay on the road, at first heaving and retching, then letting her stomach settle itself. The Fon-beast was utterly quiet, not moving at all except for a tiny tremor of the skin over his withers. At last she drank some water from her flask, gave the Singlehorn a mouthful from her palm, then went away down the long slope, pausing to rest once more at the bottom of it as she smelled the salt wind from the sea.

After a time she raised her head, habit turning her eyes to inventory the shadows. She sought them first where they had been easiest to see, along the edges of the road. None. Reluctantly, she looked behind them, seeing whether the shadows followed them only now from that battlefield at the top of the hill. None. None beneath the trees, or on the stones of the hill. None moving through the air in that lazy glide she had learned to recognize.

None. None at all.

Well, Mavin thought, it is possible. Possible they sought a certain creature; possible they found that certain creature, thus triggering some kind of feeding frenzy. Then they had fed. Would the shadows know that the creature which triggered their frenzy was not the one they ate?

Possibly not. Only possibly. Mavin wondered if they had really gone for good. She considered bringing Himaggery back again. She thought of it, meantime stroking the Fon-beast who had at last recovered his equanimity enough to tug at the halter, eager to be gone.

"No, my love," she said at last, patting him. "I can handle you better as you are. Let us come to Windlow's place and ask his help before we risk anything more. Truth to tell, Singlehorn, I am mightily weary of this journey. In all my travels across the world, I have not been this weary before. I do not know whether it is the child, or my own doubts, or you, Fonbeast, and I do not want to blame you for my weariness."

Which I might do, Himaggery. Which I would do. She had said this last silently to herself, wary of using his name. She believed the shadows were gone, but she could be wrong. Himaggery had come out of the Fon-beast shape more easily than she had expected. She would not risk it again. It would be foolish to assume . . . anything.

"I will remember what you told me, Chamferton," she vowed. "There is much I will tell Windlow when I see him at last, and there is much I will not tell Himaggery at all. Let him find some other quest to keep him busy."

They came into Hawsport on a fine, windy day, the wind straight across the wide bay from the west, carrying elusive hints of music; taran-tara and whompety-whomp. Singlehorn danced, tugging toward the shore to stand there facing the waters, adding his own voice to the melodic fragments which came over the waves.

Mavin bought meat and fruit in the market place, where children pursued the Fon-beast with offers of sweets and bits of fruit. "Is there a bridge south of here?" she asked the stallholder. "One which connects the shore with that long peninsula coming down from the north?"

"Never was that I know of," said the stallholder offhandedly, leering at her while his fingers strayed toward her thighs, making pinching motions.

Mavin drew her knife to cut a segment from a ripe thrilp and did not replace it in her belt. The stallholder became abruptly busy sorting other fruit in the pile. "No bridge there," he said, putting an end to the matter.

"Oh, yes," creaked someone from the back of the stall. "Oh, yes there was. It was built in my granddaddy's time. My granddaddy worked on it himself. They took boatloads of rock out into that shallow water and made themselves piers, they did, and put the bridge on that. Fine it was to hear him tell of it, and I heard the story many times when I was no bigger than a bunwit. It had a gate in the middle, to let the boats out, and the people used to go across it to all the western lands. . . ."

"What happened to it?" Mavin asked, ignoring the stallholder's irritation at his kinswoman's interruptions.

"Storm. A great storm. Oh, that happened when I was a child. Sixty years ago? More than that even. Such a great storm nobody had seen the like before. Half of Hawsport washed away. They say whole forests came down in the east. Dreadful thing. My granddaddy said a moon fell down. . . ."

"A moon fell down!" sneered the stallholder. "Why don't you stop with the fairy tales, Grandma. I didn't even know there was a bridge. Was you planning to go over there? My brother has a boat he rents out. Take you and the beast there in a day or so." He leered again, less hopefully.

"No," Mavin told him with a measuring look. "Can't you hear the music? The Band will need to get over here."

"The Band?" queried the old voice again. "Did you say Band? Oh, my granddaddy told me about the Band. They came through when my daddy was a boy. Before the storm, when I was just a babby, while the bridge was still there. My oh my, but I do wish I could see the Band."

"Since there is no bridge," Mavin said, "I should imagine that if the fishermen of Hawsport were to sail over to the far side, they might find a full load of paying travelers to bring back. It's only a suggestion, mind, but if the fishermen are not busy with their nets or hooks at the moment, and if they have nothing better to do. . . ."

She was speaking to vacancy. The stallholder had hurried

away toward the quay, shouting to a group of small boys
to "Go find Bettener, and Surry Bodget and the Quire
brothers. . . ."

" 'Tisn't his brother's boat at all," quavered the old voice
"He only says that to save on taxes. Pity you told him about
it. He'll only cheat those Band people, whoever they are, and
would so liked to have seen the Band."

"That's all right, Grandma," Mavin soothed her. "The
Band people have been traveling this world for a thousand
years. They probably know tricks your grandson hasn'
thought of yet. There's an old man named Byram with them
He probably remembers the moon falling down. I'll bring him
to meet you, and you two can talk about old times."

She wandered down to the shore, cutting bits of fruit for
herself and for the Fon-beast, counting the little fishing boats
which were setting out to sea. Not enough. They would have
to make two trips or more. The far peninsula lay upon the
horizon, a single dark line, as though inked in at the edge of
the ocean. The boats were tacking, to and fro, to and fro
Well, say four or five days at the outside. Time enough to rest
and eat kitcheny food. She fingered the coins in her pocket
Time enough to buy some clothing for herself. If she couldn'
Shift fur or feathers when she wished, then she would need
more than the Dervish's cast-offs to dress herself in. Time
enough to let the Fon-beast finish healing. She stroked him,
feeling his soft muzzle thrust up to nuzzle at her ear. Tempt
ing. Very tempting.

"Not until we get to Windlow's," she said. Sighing, she
went to find an inn.

Chapter 9

Mavin and the Singlehorn came to Windlow's school early of a summer evening. Though the way had been wearying, there had been no fear or horror lately, and the companionship of the Band people had replaced fear and loneliness in both their minds. Singlehorn did not shy at the sound of hunting birds any longer. Mavin did not often wake in the night starting bolt upright from dreams of gray shadows and screaming Harpies. Night was simply night once more, and day was simply day. They had come down the whole length of the shoreline from Hawsport, past the Black Basilisk Demesne, and on south to the lands of Gloam where the road turned east once more. Thence they had come up long, sloping meadows to the uplands of Brox and Brom, and there Mavin had left the Band to turn northward along the headwaters of the Long Valley River.

They left the river at last to climb eastward into the hills, and at some point in this journey, the Fon-beast began to lead them as though he knew where they were going. At least so Mavin supposed, letting him have his way. When they came over the last shallow rise looking down into Windlow's valley, she recognized it at once. Though she had never seen it, Throsset had spoken of it, and Windlow himself had described it long ago in Pfarb Durim. There was the lone white tower, and there the lower buildings which housed the students and the servants. Even from the hill she could see the sparkle of light reflecting from a fountain in the courtyard and a shower of colorful blossoms spilling over the wall.

Singlehorn gave an odd strangled but joyous call, and Mavin saw a small bent figure in the distant courtyard straighten itself and peer in their direction. Windlow was, after all, a Seer, she reminded herself. Perhaps he had expected them. If that were so, the tedious explanations she had dreaded might not be necessary. She had done things during the past season which she found it hard to justify to herself. She did not want to explain them to others.

Fon-beast led the way down the hill, tugging at the rope. She pulled him up for a moment to take off the halter, letting him gallop away toward the approaching figure. Of course he was tired of being tied. So was she. It might have been only stubbornness on her part which had insisted upon it all those last long leagues, but she had not wanted to risk his running away again. Day after day when Singlehorn had looked at her plaintively, wanting to run with the children, she had refused him. "Not again, Fon-beast. I am weary of searching for you, so you must abide the rope for a time." *However*, she had told herself, *however*, that isn't the real reason. The real reason is you would go back to that same form with him, Mavin, if you could. "You must learn to abide it," she had said aloud, ignoring the internal voices.

In time he had learned to abide it. Now that time was done. She watched his grace of movement, the flowing mane, the silken hide, knowing she had appeared the same when they had been together. They had had perfection together. Was there anything else in life which would make the loss of that bearable?

Well and no matter, she told herself. That person coming toward you is Windlow, and he is hastening his old bones at such a rate he may kill himself. Come, Mavin. Forget the past. Haste and put on a good face.

So she greeted him, and was greeted by him, and told him what person lay beneath the appearance of Singlehorn and something of what had passed, saying no more than she had to

say, and yet all in a tumble of confusing words. He passed his
hand across his face in dismay. "But in my vision, long ago, I
saw you together at Pfarb Durim!" He had aged since she saw
him last, though his eyes were as keen as she remembered
them.

"I'm sorry, Windlow. It must have been a false vision. We
did not meet in Pfarb Durim. We met in a place far to the
north, of a strangeness you will not believe when I tell it to you
over supper."

"And this is truly Himaggery?"

"It truly is."

"Is he bound in this shape forever? Is it an enchantment we
may. . . ."

"No and yes, Windlow. I will bring him out of that shape as
soon as you have heard what I must tell you." And she stub-
bornly clung to that, though Windlow said he thought she
might release Himaggery at once, and so did Boldery, who was
there on a visit, and so did Throsset of Dowes who was like-
wise.

"I will tell *you*," she said to Windlow, granting no com-
promise. "And then I will release Himaggery and all of you
may say whatever you like to him and may tell him everything
he should know. When he has had a chance to think about it
all—why, then he and I will talk. . . ."

"I don't understand," said Boldery in confusion. "Why
won't she bring him back to himself now?"

"Let her alone," Throsset directed, unexpectedly. "I imagine she has had a wearying time. It will not matter in the
long run."

So there was one more meal with Himaggery lying on the
hearth in his Singlehorn guise during which Mavin told them
all that she knew or guessed or had been told about Himaggery's quest and subsequent captivity, carefully not telling
them where the Dervish's valley was, or what had happened to
her there, or where she had seen the tower.

"Chamferton says Himaggery must leave it alone," she
concluded. "I believe him. The shadows did seek Himaggery,
and it was a great part luck and only by the narrowest edge
that they did not eat us both. The shadows fed upon Pantiquod and her sisters and did not seem to know the difference,

but I would not face such a peril again—not willingly." The telling of it still had the power to bring it back, and her body shook again with revulsion and terror. Throsset put a hand upon hers, looking oddly at her, as though she had seen more than Mavin had said. Mavin put down her empty wineglass and rose to her feet, swaying a little at the cumulative effect of wine, weariness, and having attained the long awaited goal. Her voice was not quite steady as she said, "Now, I have told you everything, Windlow. I will do as I promised."

She laid her cheek briefly against Singlehorn's soft nose. "Come out, Himaggery," she said, turning away without waiting to see whether the words had any effect. She left the room, shutting the door, while behind her a man struggled mightily with much confusion of spirit and in answer to a beloved voice, to bring himself out of the Singlehorn form and to remain upright on tottery human legs. For Mavin, there was a soft bed waiting in a tower room, and she did not intend to get out of it for several days.

The knock came on her door late, so late that she had forgotten what time it was or where she was, or that she was. Aroused out of dream, she heard the whisper, "Mavin, are you asleep?" and answered truthfully. "Yes. Yes I am." Whoever it was went away. When she woke in the morning, very late, she thought it might have been Windlow. Or perhaps Himaggery.

She had bought clothing in Hawsport, during the days spent there waiting for the Band to be ferried over from the peninsula. Skirts—she remembered skirts from Pfarb Durim a time before—and an embroidered tunic, cut low, and a stiff belt of gilded leather to make her waist look small, though indeed it was already tighter than when she had bought it. When she was fully awake—it might have been the following day or several days, she didn't know—and after a long luxurious washing of body and hair, she dressed herself in this unaccustomed finery and went into Windlow's garden.

Someone observed her seated there and went to tell someone else. After a time she heard halting steps upon the stone and turned to find him there, neatly trimmed of hair and beard, walking toward her with the hesitant stride he was to have for some years, as any four-footed creature might if hoisted high upon two legs and told to stay there.

She was moved to see him so familiar, as she had pictured him a thousand times. "Himaggery. For a time, you know, I had not thought to set eyes upon you in human shape again." She was unprepared for his tears, and forgave him that he was not her silken-maned lover any longer.

They sat in the garden for some time, hours, talking and not talking. He had heard of the journey and was content to ask few questions about it.

She was less content. "Do you remember anything at all about being the Singlehorn?" she asked. "Do you remember anything at all about the Dervish's valley?"

He turned very pale. "No. And yet . . . sometimes I dream about it. But I can't remember, after I've wakened, what the dream was about."

She kept her voice carefully noncommittal. "Do you desire to return there?"

"I don't think so," he faltered. "But . . . it would be good to run, I think. As I ran. As we ran. We were there together, weren't we?"

She waited, hoping he would go on to speak of that time, even a few words. He said nothing more. After a time he began to talk about other things, about plans for his future, things he might do. He asked about the Lake of Faces, and she described it as she had seen it in moonlight, with the Harpy questioning the Faces. She told him of Rose-love's answer, and of the man who spoke of the Great Game taking place around Lake Yost. This piqued his interest, for he remembered the place, and they spoke for a time comfortably about things which did not touch them too closely.

When the bell rang to tell them supper was served in the tower, he took her hand and would not let her go. "May I come to your room tonight?" Not looking at her, dignified and yet prepared for her refusal, hardly daring to ask her and yet not daring to go without asking. She was more moved by that pathetic dignity than she would have been by any importunate pleas.

"Of course. I hoped you would." That, at least, had been

the truth. Later, deep in the ecstatic night, she knew it was still the truth, and more than the truth.

Several days later she sat with Throsset in that same tower room, lying upon a pile of pillows, a basket of fruit at her side. Throsset had been nervously stalking about for some minutes, picking things up and putting them down. Now she cleared her throat and said, "You're pregnant, aren't you? I've been watching you for days. All that nonsense on the road with those Harpies! Any Shifter worth a trip through the p'natti could have handled a dozen Harpies without being touched. But you didn't Shift. You haven't Shifted once since you've been here. Not even to fit yourself to a chair or lie comfortably before the fire. How far along are you?"

"I don't know," Mavin replied, almost in a whisper. "I was Shifted when it happened, not myself. In the Dervish's valley. It could have been a season I was there with him, or a few days. I don't know." She did not mention the time she had visited that valley eight years before. She wondered if Himaggery would ever remember how it had been, they two together in the valley. Somehow it seemed terribly important that he remember it—without being reminded of it.

"Shifted when it happened! Well and well, Mavin. That leaves me wondering much. Time was we would have assumed it an ill thing and believed that no good issue could come of it. I'm not certain of that any more. Still it's interesting. And you don't know how long ago? Well, we can figure it out. I left you near Pfarb Durim early in the season of storms. You traveled from there how many days before you found him?"

Mavin counted. "One to the Lake of Faces. One to Chamferton's tower—or to him who said he was Chamferton. I don't know after that, three or four days, I think, following the runners. Perhaps two days to find the Dervish, then time got lost."

"So, the earliest it could have happened would have been still during the season of storms. Only a few days after you left me. Then how long to come south?"

"Forever, Throsset. Days at Chamferton's tower, straightening out that mess. Days searching for Singlehorn. Days running from shadows. Days trying to hide from Pantiquod, until the shadows ate her. Days and more days following the Band as it came south along the shore. Days following the river courses. Then across country, through the mountains. To here. And the time here, these last few days."

"So. Perhaps about one hundred days ago. Perhaps a bit more. Not really showing yet, but I can tell that you feel it. Any Shifter-woman can feel it almost from the beginning, of course. A kind of foreign presence telling one not to Shift."

"You have had . . . "

"Two. A son, a daughter. Long ago. Neither were Shifter, so after they came of age I left them with their father's kin. Better that way. Still, sometimes . . . "

"Did you use a forgetter?"

"Of course not. They were grown, and fond enough of me. They forget soon enough on their own, and if they're ever ashamed of having a Shifter mother, then bad luck to them." She laughed harshly enough to show that the thought of this hurt her. "What are you going to do?"

"Do?"

"Do. Are you going to stay with Himaggery? He wants you to go with him to build a great demesne at that place he talks of, near Lake Yost. The place with unlimited power. He says anything is possible to one with a demesne at such a place."

"And if I go with him, what?" Mavin asked in a bleak voice. Then, rising to stride about, her voice becoming a chanting croon in the firelight. "When I think of him, Throsset, I am afire to be with him. My skin aches for him. It is only soothed when I am pressed tight against him, as tight as we can manage. My nipples keep pushing against my clothes, wanting out, wanting him to touch them. Then, when we are together, we make love and lie side by side, our arms twisted together, and there is such wonderful peace, like floating— quiet and dusky, with no desires for a time. And then he talks of his plans. His plans, his desires, his philosophy. Of things he has read. I listen. Sometimes I think he is very naive, for I have found things in the world to be different from his beliefs, but he does not hear me if I say so.

"So I merely listen. I fall asleep. Or, if not, my head starts to hurt. Soon I ache to be away, in some quiet place with the wind calling, or in some wild storm where I could fly, run, move. And so I go into the woods and am peaceful away from him for a time, until I am brought back like a fish upon a line. . . .

"If I go with him, what?" she asked. "I keep asking myself that. He has never asked me what I would like to do."

"That's not true," objected Throsset, "I heard him ask you as we dined last evening. . . ."

"You heard him ask me, and if you listened, you heard him answer his own question and go on talking. He asked me what I would like to do, and then he told me how useful a Shifter would be to him. He has heard the story of our journey south, but he has not questioned why I could not Shift. He has not questioned why I have not Shifted in the time we have been here."

"That's true," Throsset sighed. "Men sometimes do not see these things."

"So." Mavin nodded. "Since they do not see these things, if I were to go with him, then what?"

"You're planning to go to Lake Yost, aren't you," Windlow asked Himaggery. "You haven't stopped talking about it since you first heard about the place. Not even when you're with Mavin, at least not while the two of you are with anyone else. Why all this sudden interest in the place?"

"At first I was afire to go back north," Himaggery said, laying the pen to one side and shuffling his papers together. "Couldn't wait to try that tower again. I figured out how I got caught the first time, and I had all sorts of ideas that might have worked to outwit the shadows—or distract them. I don't think they have 'wits' in the sense we mean. But the longer I thought about it, the more I decided you were right, Windlow. The time isn't right for it. So, the next best thing is to set up the kind of demesne you and I have talked of from time to time. And an excellent place to do it is at Lake Yost. There's more power there than any collection of Gamesmen can use in a thousand years, enough to make the place the strongest fortress in the lands of the True Game."

"Mavin told you the place has been emptied?"

"She learned of it at the Lake of Faces. Actually, I already knew of Lake Yost. A marvelous location but it was held by a troop of idiots, True Game fanatics, wanting only to challenge and play, come what might of it. They called Great Game a season ago, a Game so large we haven't seen its like in a decade. With the unlimited power of the place, they succeeded in killing all the players, every Gamesman. The place is emptied and dead, ready for my taking."

"And will Mavin go with you?"

"Of course! We can't lose one another now, not after all this time."

Windlow went to the tower window, stood there watching the clouds move slowly over the long meadows to the west. There were shadows beneath them on the grasses, and he wondered if *the* shadows hid in these harmless places unseen, when they did not wish to be seen. "Have you thought she might have something else she would like to do?"

"Ah, but what could be more important than this, old teacher? Eh? A place where your ideas can be taught? A place where we can bring together Gamesmen who believe in those words of yours, where we can work together! Wouldn't anyone want to be part of that?"

"Not everyone, my boy. No. There are many who would not want to be part of that, and that doesn't make them villains, either."

"Mavin will want to come with me," he said with satisfaction. "Windlow, we are so in love. I imagined it, all those years, but I could not imagine even a fraction of it. She wouldn't lose that anymore than I would."

"You've asked her, I presume."

"Of course I have! What do you take me for, old teacher? Some kind of barbarian? Kings and other Beguilers may hold unwilling followers—or followers who would be unwilling if they were in their own minds—but Wizards do not. At least this Wizard does not."

"I just wondered if it had occurred to you—a thought I've had from time to time, a passing thing, you know—that love behaves much as Beguilement does. Mertyn, for example. Do you remember him at all?

"Mavin's brother. Surely I remember him. A nice child.

Boldery's friend. Of course, he was only eleven or twelve when I left the School, so I don't remember him well. . . ."

"Mertyn had the Talent of Beguilement, you know. Had it early, as a fifteen-season child, I think. And it was Mertyn who kept Mavin's sister from leaving the place they lived, not a very pleasant place for women to hear Mertyn tell of it. He blamed himself, you know, crying over it in the night sometimes. And I asked him if his sister loved him, even without the Beguilement, and he told me yes, she did. So—mostly to relieve the child's mind, you understand—I said it could have been love did it just as well. And he was not responsible for that. We may be responsible for those we love, but hardly ever for those who love us. Takes a saint to do that." He turned from this slow, ruminative speech to find Himaggery's eyes fixed on some point in space. "Himaggery?"

"Um? Oh, sorry. I was thinking about Lake Yost. There's a perfect site for a community, as I recall, near the place the hot springs come up. I was trying to remember whether there was a little bay there. It seems to me there was, but it's not clear. You were saying?" He turned his smiling face toward the old man, eyes alight but already shifting again toward that distant focus.

"Nothing," Windlow sighed. "Nothing, Himaggery. Perhaps we'll talk about it some other time."

"I wanted you to have this account of the Eesties," said Mavin, handing the sheets of parchment to the old man. "Foolishly, I betrayed myself into giving one such account to the false Chamferton. He was very excited over it. I think he would have tried to hold me in some dungeon or other if I hadn't cooperated with him so willingly."

She sat upon the windowsill of the tower room, waiting while he read them over, hearing his soft exclamations of delighted interest, far different from Chamferton's crow of victory when he received his copy. The washerwomen were working at the long trough beside the well, and a fat, half-naked baby staggered among them, dabbling in the spilled water. She considered this mite, half in wonder, half in apprehension.

"And you can't speak of this at all?" Windlow asked at last.

"Not at all," she said. "And yet nothing prevents my writing it down."

"Let's see," he murmured, "You went to Ganver's Grave and . . . ahau, ghaaa . . ." He choked, coughed, grasped at his throat as though something were caught there, panted, glared around himself in panic. Mavin darted to him, held him up and quiet as the attack passed. He sat down, put his head upon his folded arms. "Frightening," he whispered. "Utterly frightening. The geas is laid not only upon you, then, but upon anyone?"

"To speak of it, yes. But not to write of it. That fact makes me wonder strangely."

"For a start, it makes me wonder if the . . . they do not choose to be spoken of by the ignorant. They don't mind being read of by literate people, however. Remarkable."

"I thought so, too," she agreed. "Except that the pawns have a thousand fables about the rolling stars and the Old Ones and the Eesties. Nothing stops their throats. Nothing stopped old Rose-love when she told me the story of Weetzie and the daylight bell."

"Because fables are fables." He nodded, ticking the points off to himself. "And facts are facts. You could probably tell the story of your own meeting with them, Mavin, if you fabulized it."

"Girl-shifter and the Crimson Egg," she laughed. "The story of Fustigar-woman and the shadowpeople."

"Quite wonderful. Are you going back there? Seeking the Eesties again?"

"Of course," she cried in unconscious delight of which Windlow was altogether conscious. "Who could not? Oh, Windlow, you would like that place. As full of marvels as a shell is full of egg. And there are other things, things having nothing to do with the Eesties. There's a place below the ridge by Schlaizy Noithn like nothing you have ever seen. I call it the Blot. Traders come there—Traders some say. I think them false gifters, myself—and I want to explore it one day. And I left a girl-child friend across the sea. Her I would see again, before I am old, her and her children."

"And what about your child?" he asked, head cocked to one side, gentle as the wind as he said it.

"How did you know?"

He shrugged. "Oh, I'm a Seer, Mavin. Of one thing and another. In this case, however, it was a case of using my mind and my heart, nothing more. Himaggery doesn't know, does he?"

"Anyone might know," she replied in a sober voice. "Anyone who used mind or heart. Throsset knew."

"You won't allow that he's simply afire to get on with his life, so much of it having been spent in a kind of sleep?"

"Why, of course!" she answered in exasperation. "Why, of course I'll allow it. Do I constrain him to do other than he will? He lost eight years in that valley. Should I demand he turn from his life to look at me? Or listen to me? Windlow. That's not the question to ask, and you know it."

He nodded, rather sadly, getting up with a groan and a thud of his stick upon the floor. "Surely, Mavin. Surely. Well. Since it seems you'll not be Shifting for a time—do I have it right? That is the custom? More than custom, perhaps?—call upon me for whatever you need. Midwives perhaps, when the time comes? I have little power but many good friends."

"I do not know yet what I will need, old sir. Midwives, I guess, though whether here or elsewhere, I cannot say."

"You'll risk that, will you?"

"Risk Midwives? I would not do other. It is a very good thing the Midwives do, to look into the future of each child to see whether it will gain a soul or not. The great houses may scoff at Midwives if they will, caring not that their soulless children make wreck and ruin upon the earth. Of such houses are Ghouls born, Gamesmen like Blourbast and Huld the Demon." She did not mention Huld's son, Mandor. Years later, deep in the caves beneath Bannerwell, she was to curse herself for that omission. If Windlow had known of Mandor . . . if Mertyn had known of Mandor . . . "Of course I will risk Midwives, and count the risk well taken to know I have born no soulless wight who may grow to scourge the earth and the company of men."

He smiled then, taking her hand in his own and leaning to

kiss her on the cheek, a sweet, old man's kiss with much kindness in it. "Mavin, perhaps I erred when I had that vision of you and Himaggery in Pfarb Durim. It seems to me that in that vision your hair was gray. Perhaps it was meant to be later, that's all." He sighed. "Whatever you need, Mavin. Tell me." Then they left the place and went to their lunch, spread on a table in the courtyard among the herb pots and the garden flowers. For a quiet time in that garden, Mavin told herself she would stay where she was, for the peace of it was pleasant and as kindly as old Windlow's kiss.

"You might remember that he's eight years younger than he seems," commented Throsset. "All that time in the valley. He didn't live then, really. In fact, he may have gone backwards. . . ."

"To become what?" Mavin asked, examining her face in the mirror. She had never before been very interested in her own face, but now it fascinated her. One of Windlow's servant girls had asked if she could arrange Mavin's hair, and the piled, sculptured wealth of it made her look unlike herself. "Become a child, you mean?"

Throsset swung her feet, banging her heels cheerfully against the wall below the windowsill where she sat, half over the courtyard, defying gravity and dignity at once as she tempted the laundress's boy-child with a perfect target for his peashooter. "Children are very self-centered, Mavin. They are so busy learning about themselves, you know, that they have no time for anything else. You were like that, I'm sure. I know I was. Himaggery, on the other hand, went straight from his family demesne into Windlow's school, and straight from that into continuous study—books, collections. Not Gaming. Not paying attention to other people, you know."

" 'Among,' but not 'of,' " commented Mavin, touching the corner of her eyes with a finger dipped in dust-of-blue. She turned. "Do you like that? It's interesting."

"I like the brown better," Throsset advised. "Better with your skin. What are you up to with these pawn tricks, anyhow?"

Mavin turned back to the mirror, wiping away the blue stain to replace it with dust-of-brown. She had bought the tiny cosmetic jars from a traveling Trader and was being self-consciously experimental with them. "I'm finding out whether I can get him to look at me."

"He looks at you all the time. He's in love with you."

"I mean see me. He doesn't care whether I'm Mavin the woman, a fustigar hunting bunwits, or a Singlehorn. He's in love with his idea of me." She applied a bit more of the brown shadow, then picked up the tiny brush to blind herself painting her lashes.

"Your eyelashes are all right!" Throsset thumped down from the window, brushing at her seat, not seeing the pea which shot through the opening behind her. "When are you going to tell him?"

"I'm not." She was definite about this. "And you're not to tell him either."

"Oh, Mavin, by all the hundred devils but you're difficult. Why not?"

"Because, dear Fairy Godmother"—The proper designation for one with both Shifting and Sorcery was "Fairy Godmother." Mavin had looked it up in the Index and had been perversely waiting for an occasion to use it. Now she took wicked pleasure in Throsset's discomfiture—"*dear* Fairy Godmother, what you saw and what Windlow saw you saw by observation. Himaggery is no innocent. He knows where babies come from. He does know we were together in the Valley. It is a kind of test, my dear, which may be unfair, but it is nonetheless a test I am determined to use."

"And if he passes it?"

"If *he* passes it, with no advice from either you or Windlow —whom I have been at some pains to silence—then I will go with him to Lake Yost, and see what it is he plans to do there with his thousand good Gamesmen. And I will not Mavin at him, will not flee from him, will not distress him."

"And if he fails . . ."

"Then, Throsset of Dowes, I will know that it really does not matter to him much. He is in love with the idea of me, and that idea will content him. He will be reasonably satisfied with memory and hope and a brave resolution to find me once again—which he will put off from season to season, since there will always be other things to do." She looked up at

Throsset with a quirk of the eyebrows. "Listen to me, Throsset, for I have made a discovery. It may be that Himaggery will *prefer* the idea of me to the reality—*prefer* to remember me with much romantic, sentimental recollection, at his convenience, as when a sweetly painted sky seems to call for such feelings of gentle melancholy. In the evenings, perhaps, when the sun is dropping among long shadows and the air breathes sadness. On moonlit nights, with the trees all silvered . . .

"A remembered love, Throsset of Dowes, does not interfere with one's work! A lovely, lost romance is a convenience for any busy man!"

"You're cynical. And footloose. You simply don't want to sit still long enough to rear this child."

"I'll sit still, Throsset! Where I will and when I will, and for as long as is necessary. And if Himaggery sees the meaning behind this paint on my face or realizes I am carrying his child, well then I will become dutiful, Throsset. So dutiful, even Danderbat Keep would have been pleased." She made a face, then rummaged in her jewel box for some sparkling something to put in her hair. "I have discovered something else, Throsset of Dowes. And that is that men give women jewels when they have absolutely no idea what might please them and are not willing to take time to think about it."

They sat beside the fountain beneath the stars. Out in the meadow other stars bobbled and danced, lantern bugs dizzying among the grasses.

"I used to imagine this," said Himaggery. She lay half in his lap, against his chest, watching the lights, half asleep after a long, warm and lazy day.

"What did you imagine? Sitting under the sky watching bugs dance?"

"No, silly. I imagined you. And me. Together. Here or somewhere like here. I knew how it would be."

"This isn't how it would be," she said, the words flowing out before she could stop them. "This is an interlude, a sweet season. It's no more real than . . . than we were before, in the valley."

"How can you say that?" He laughed, somewhat uneasily. "You're real. I'm real. In our own shapes, our own minds."

She shook her head. Now that she had started, she had to go on. "No, love. I'm in *a* shape, a courtyard shape, a lover's shape, a pretty girl shape, a romantic evening shape. I have other shapes for other times. With those other shapes, it would be a different thing...."

"Not at all. No matter what shape it might be, it would always be you inside it!" His vehemence hid apprehension. She could smell it.

She soothed him. "Himaggery, let me tell you a story.

"Far on the western edge of the land, there's a town I visited once. Pleasant people there. One charming girl-child I fell in love with. About nine years old, I suppose, full of joy and bounce and love. She was killed by a man of the town, a Wolf. Everyone knew it. They couldn't prove it. They had locked him up for such things before, but had always let him go. It was expensive to keep him locked up and guarded, and fed and warm. It took bread from their own mouths to keep him locked away...."

"What has this to do with..." he began. She shushed him.

"So, though everyone knew he had done it, no one did anything except walk fearfully and lock up their children. I was not satisfied with that. I took the shape of one of his intended victims, Himaggery, and I ended the matter."

There was a long pause. She heard him swallow, sigh. "As I would have done, too, Mavin, had I the Talent. I do not dispute your judgment."

"You don't. Well, the people of the town suspected I might have had something to do with it, and one of them came to remonstrate with me that such a course of action was improper. So I asked why they had not kept him locked up, or killed him the first time they had proof, and they told me it would have been cruel to do so. And I asked then if it were not cruel to their children to let the Wolf run loose among them. They did not answer me.

"So then, Himaggery, I took their children away from them. All. Far to the places of the True Game. For at least in the lands of the True Game people are not such hypocrites. I thought better those children chance a hazardous life knowing who their enemies were than to live in that town where their own people conspired with their butchers.''

There was another long silence. "You were very upset at the child's death,'' he said at last.

"Yes. Very.''

"So you were not yourself. If you had had time to think, to reflect, you would not have acted so.''

Then she was silent. At last she said with a sigh, "No, Himaggery, I was myself. Completely myself. And if I'd had longer to think on it, I would have done worse.''

He tried to tell her she was merely tired, but she changed the subject to something light and laugh-filled. Later they made love under the stars. It was the last conversation they had together.

Midmorning of the following day, Throsset of Dowes rode with Mavin northward along the meadow edge. They had brought some food and wine with them, intending to take a meal upon the grassy summit which overlooked the canyon lands before Throsset left for the south. Throsset had decided to go visiting her children soon, away in the Sealands. It was a sudden decision.

"I decided they would scarcely remember me unless I went soon. I haven't gone before because I feared they would reject me, a Shifter. But if I don't go, then I have rejected them. So better let the fault lie upon their heads if it must lie anywhere. I will go south tomorrow. I have not run in fustigar shape for a season and a half, not since I met you outside Pfarb Durim. I am getting fat and lazy.''

Mavin hugged her. "You will be here tonight then? Good. You will be able to tell them that I have gone.''

"Ah,'' said Throsset, a little sadly. "Well. So you have made up your mind.''

"When we have had our lunch, you will ride back and I will ride on. Tell Windlow I will repay him for the horse sometime.''

"Windlow would have given you the horse. Where are you going? Why are you going?''

"I am going because I do not want this child to be born here, or at Lake Yost, to serve as a halter strap between me and Himaggery. I am going because Himaggery does not see me as I am, and I cannot be what he thinks I am. I am going because there is much distraction here, of a wondrous kind, and I want two years, or three, to give to the child without distractions.

"As to where. Well. North. Somewhere. I have friends there. I will find Midwives there. And when the time is right, I may see Himaggery again. Windlow now thinks his vision was of a later time. We may yet come together in Pfarb Durim."

"What am I to tell them?"

"That I became restless. That I have gone on a journey. Don't say much more than that. Himaggery will be quite happy with that. Each day he will think of going off to find me. Each day he will put it off for a while. Each night he will dream romantic dreams of me, and each morning he will resolve again—quite contentedly.

"Don't tell him I'm expecting a child. If he knew, he would first have to decide how to feel about it, and then what actions such a feeling should create. Better leave him as he is. After all, the Midwives may not let the child live. So don't take his smile from him, Throsset. Strangely though I seem to show it, I do love him."

They drank the wine. When they had done, Throsset threw the jug against a stone, shattering it into pieces. She wrote her name upon a shard and gave it to Mavin, accepting a similar one in return. So were meetings and partings memorialized among their people, without tears.

After Mavin rode down into the canyon lands, Throsset sat for a long time staring after her. She was not sad, not gay, not grieving or rejoicing. She went boneless and did the quick wriggle which passed for comment in Danderbat Keep; Mavin could not Shift for a time, but she was still Mavin Manyshaped, and Throsset did not doubt she would return.

"Good chance to you," she whispered toward the north. "And to your child, Mavin." Nothing answered but the wind. Putting the shard into her pocket as one of the few things she would always carry, she went to tell them that Mavin Manyshaped had gone.

Fantasy from Ace
fanciful and fantastic!

COLLECTIONS OF FANTASY AND SCIENCE FICTION

Stories
~ of ~
Swords and Sorcery

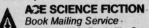